The Famous Five Go On Television

A new adventure of the
characters created by
Enid Blyton, told by Claude
Voilier, translated by
Anthea Bell

Illustrated by John Cooper

KNIGHT BOOKS
Hodder and Stoughton

Copyright © Librairie Hachette 1973
First published in France as *Les Cinq a la Television*
English language translation copyright © Hodder and Stoughton Ltd. 1981
Illustrations copyright © Hodder and Stoughton Ltd. 1981

First published in Great Britain by Knight Books 1981
Sixth impression 1985

British Library C.I.P.

Voilier, Claude
     The Famous Five go on television.
     I. Title
     843'.914[J]   PZ7

     ISBN 0-340-27247-3

Printed and bound in Great Britain for Hodder and Stoughton Paperbacks, a division of Hodder and Stoughton Ltd., Mill Road, Dunton Green, Sevenoaks, Kent (Editorial Office: 47 Bedford Square, London, WC1 3DP) by Hunt Barnard Printing Ltd., Aylesbury, Bucks.

CONTENTS

Chapter One

A VERY SPECIAL HOLIDAY

'Oh, come on, George! Hand over that newspaper, do!'

Just to tease her cousins, Julian, Dick and Anne, George pretended that she hadn't heard what they were saying. She made out that she was absorbed in reading the newspaper in front of her – until Dick snatched it away.

'My word!' he cried, after a quick glance at it. 'We've made front page news! We're famous!'

'We were famous already!' said George. 'Weren't we, Timmy?'

'Woof!' replied Timmy the dog, jumping up at his mistress. He and George were inseparable companions!

Julian and Anne bent their own fair heads over the page. It showed a big picture of the four children and Timmy, with a caption underneath saying, 'The Famous Five! Thanks to these children and their dog, the Falcon Gang of cigarette smugglers has just been arrested!'

It was not by any means the first time George,

her three cousins and Timmy had found themselves in the news. They had already had a great many adventures, and even solved several mysteries which baffled the police! Without the Five, Sir Donald Riddington would never have got his valuable collection of watches back, and Professor Hayling and his son Tinker wouldn't have seen their pet cheetah again. The newspaper mentioned both these adventures, as well as several other cases in which the Five had been involved.

The four cousins were out in the garden of Kirrin Cottage, which belonged to George's parents, Uncle Quentin and Aunt Fanny. The weather was mild, although it was winter – the Christmas holidays were nearly over. Suddenly Uncle Quentin appeared in the doorway of the house. George's father was a very clever scientist, who was always deep in his work and was usually rather strict with the children. But today he was smiling.

'I've got some good news for you!' he told them. 'Next April I have to go to a scientific conference at Southbourne. It's during the Easter holidays, and so I thought I'd take you too, for a very special holiday. It's a reward for solving that smuggling mystery and helping the police! Southbourne is a lovely place, with lots of things to do, so it will be quite a change for you. Aunt Fanny will tell you all the details. But mind – you won't be coming unless you get good reports next term!'

And Uncle Quentin went back indoors,

leaving the children feeling very excited.

'Three cheers for Uncle Quentin!' shouted Dick.

'Hip, hip, hooray!' cried George. 'I know Father and I don't always see eye to eye, but all the same I'm very fond of him!'

'And Aunt Fanny is a dear, too!' added Anne.

'Just think of having to wait another three months!' sighed Julian. 'Still, it can be lovely further along the coast in April!'

* * *

That term went by faster than the children had expected. And as they *did* get good reports from their schools, Uncle Quentin kept his promise. He arranged for all the Five to spend the Easter holidays in Southbourne. Julian, who was very responsible for his age, had the job of looking after the other children on the journey. George and Dick, who were quite close to each other in age, were both very lively, and were quite a handful! Then there was Anne – but though she was the youngest of the children, only just ten, she was always good. 'Almost too good to be true!' George sometimes said.

When they reached Southbourne, Julian organised a taxi to take them to the Rose Hotel, a marvellous luxury hotel near the centre of the town. A porter, dressed in a smart green and gold uniform, showed them to the rooms which Uncle Quentin had reserved. Aunt Fanny and Uncle

Quentin were already there. Dick and Julian were pleased to find their room had a balcony overlooking the sea.

'Look, we've got a shower in our bathroom,' said George exploring the room which she and Anne were to share.

Anne found that there was a little kettle, with things to make tea and coffee. 'Good,' she said, pleased, 'I'll be able to make us a drink whenever we want one.'

Timmy barked to show his approval. He liked the look of the basket which had been placed in the corner of the room.

When they had unpacked, Aunt Fanny told the children they could go and stretch their legs on the promenade along the sea front. The Five, in happy holiday mood, thought that was a terrific idea, and hurried off.

The four cousins were delighted to see the sea again. They thought it looked quite different here from the seaside near Kirrin which they knew so well! There were all kinds of boats bobbing about in the bay – and some magnificent yachts which the children thought must belong to very rich people indeed. As for Timmy, *he* seemed more interested in the seagulls. He started chasing them, much to the amusement of the people on the promenade. The seagulls were very tame, and went about pecking at breadcrumbs. They let the dog come quite close and then flew up, right under his nose, screeching! It sounded as if they were saying something rude to poor Timmy.

'Oh, do stop, Timmy!' cried George, laughing. 'People will notice us!'

But someone already had noticed them – a young man who came up to the children.

'I thought so!' he said. 'Aren't you the Famous Five who were in all the papers last Christmas?'

Pleased to be recognised, Dick grinned broadly at the man.

'That's right!' he said, trying to sound modest but not being very successful! 'Yes, we're the Five!'

Then the stranger explained that he worked for the local radio and television station. He asked the children if they would be staying in Southbourne long.

'Only while my father's attending a conference being held here,' George told him. 'It's going to last about a fortnight.'

The young man seemed to be thinking over what she had said. Then he smiled. 'Listen – how would you like to be on television?' he asked. 'Now that I've been lucky enough to meet you, I've had a marvellous idea! But I must consult the people at the studios – just write your address in Southbourne down here, and you may soon be hearing from me!'

And he disappeared before the four cousins could get over their surprise!

Anne was rather worried. 'Do you think he's mad?' she asked.

'No!' said Dick. 'I think he's a practical joker!'

'I think he was perfectly serious, myself,' said George. 'But he forgot to tell us his name.'

'Yes, that's odd,' Julian agreed. 'Well, all we can do is wait and see what happens.'

By the time they sat down to supper that evening, the children had forgotten their meeting with the stranger. After the meal, however, they were following Uncle Quentin and Aunt Fanny through the hall of the hotel when the manageress came along.

'There's a gentleman here to see you, sir,' she told Uncle Quentin. 'Here's his card.'

Uncle Quentin took the little card and read out loud, 'Ralph Morris, Producer and Director, South-East Television.'

'Good gracious!' he exclaimed. 'I wonder what on earth he wants? I've never met him in my life!'

But a tall young man was already coming towards them, smiling. Yes – it was the man the children had met on the promenade!

'May I have a word with you, sir? It's about these chidren! The newspapers were full of them last winter, and meeting them by chance this afternoon I got the idea of making a television film in several episodes about their latest adventure. Would you care to talk it over with me?'

They all went into the hotel lounge. The children listened, thrilled, as Ralph Morris explained what he wanted to do.

'I've been consulting the studio management, sir, and we'd like to make the film as a serial telling the story of the Five and the Falcon Gang, and how the smugglers were brought to justice. As the representative of South-East Television,

I'm authorised to make what I hope you'll think a handsome offer!'

'Oh, that doesn't worry me!' Uncle Quentin said at once. 'But I'm not so sure I like the idea of all this publicity for my daughter and her cousins. Besides –'

'Oh, Father!' George interrupted eagerly. 'We'd have such fun!'

'And I'd love to get first-hand experience of the way television films are actually made!' added Julian, his eyes sparkling. 'It would be very – very *educational*, don't you think Uncle Quentin?'

Uncle Quentin started to laugh. 'Educational, eh? You certainly know how to get round me, you young scoundrel! All right, all right! But I must have guarantees that you'll be safe and well looked after.'

'I'll be personally responsible for the young people, sir,' Ralph Morris told him. 'I shall be directing the film myself, so I'll keep an eye on them all the time. You needn't worry!'

Then there was a long business discussion – but the children hardly listened to that, they were so excited. This very special holiday was going to be even more fun than they'd expected!

They only started paying real attention again when they heard Ralph Morris saying that a rough draft of the televison script was being written at that very moment. Most of the indoor scenes, he said, would be filmed at South-East Television's studios, while the outdoor scenes would be shot 'on location'. Luckily there were several places near Southbourne where the coast looked quite like the seaside near Kirrin. And the shooting of the film was to begin in just two days' time!

Chapter Two

THE TELEVISION STUDIOS

So two days later, quite early in the morning, a car from the television studios came to fetch the children and Timmy. South-East Television had a big, modern building. Ralph Morris himself came out to welcome the children. They thought the luxurious offices were wonderful, and they were fascinated by all the cameras and the sound recording equipment. It was really interesting! Looking through a glass panel, Anne watched a scene being filmed on what was called a 'set' the other side. She was a little scared.

'I'll never *dare* act in front of the cameras!' she said.

George gave her cousin a friendly thump on the back.

'Don't be an ass! This is a wonderful opportunity – think of us making a real film. It's going to be great fun, you wait and see!'

Ralph Morris took the Five into his own big office, where they met several other people. He told them that these were the professional actors who were to play parts in the film about the Five and the Falcon Gang.

Everyone was introduced. A well-known actor called Steve Vane was to play Joe Falcon, the dashing leader of the smugglers' gang. Three other actors, whose names were Mark Turner, John Ferris and Emlyn Jones, were going to be the members of the gang, and there was an actress too – a pretty young woman called Suzy Marshall.

Smiling, she shook hands with the children – and then shook paws with Timmy.

'In the film, I'm Mrs Falcon, Joe's wife,' she told the children. 'And in fact Steve and I are engaged to be married in real life!'

Julian, Dick, Anne and George were thrilled by all of this. They liked the actors very much and were pleased to think they would be working together.

Ralph Morris lost no time in getting his company ready to start filming. They were to begin in the studios.

'You see,' he explained to the children, 'we don't shoot the separate scenes in the order in which they'll appear in the story. We do several of the indoor scenes together, in the studio, and then several scenes on location – it's more economical that way. Today, all you'll have to do is watch the others acting, just to give you the idea. It'll be your turn to go in front of the cameras tomorrow. Don't worry; everything will be fine! We have to make this film in a very short time, because you're

16

George gave her cousin a friendly thump on the back – 'Don't be an ass!'

Julian, Dick, Anne and George liked the actors very much.

only here in Southbourne for a fortnight. It's an action-packed story, and I want to keep the suspense going right to the end!'

The shooting of the film began with a scene where the smugglers' gang met. Julian, Dick, George and Anne watched the actors closely. Ralph Morris felt sure the children themselves would all be 'naturals' in front of the cameras. He wasn't worried about that part of it – or not nearly as worried as they were!

After this scene, Ralph shot a short bit of film of the Five, just as a trial run. Everything went perfectly, exactly as he had expected!

The children spent that afternoon learning their lines off by heart for the next day, and being shown how to move around on the set and speak into the microphone. By now, George and her cousins felt as if they had known the television actors for ages.

'They're awfully nice,' said Anne.

'Very friendly, too!' remarked Julian.

'I like Steve a lot,' said Dick.

George, who was very observant, had already noticed the different actors' little ways. Steve, for instance, had a habit of tossing back a lock of his hair, while Suzy was always starting her sentences with the words, 'If you ask me . . .'. And Mark, who was Steve's cousin, was obviously very fond of a particular brand of peppermints – as he was always sucking them, and said they were very good, though it wasn't easy to get hold of this brand. He gave the children some.

Next day the Five got down to real work, acting

a dramatic scene from their own adventure! It was filmed in a cave made of polystyrene inside the studio. It looked quite convincing. The smugglers had kept the children prisoner in this cave, but Timmy got on their track, and helped George undo the ropes which held her, so that she could set her cousins free.

'Right – we're shooting now!' Ralph Morris told them.

Tied hand and foot in the dim, greenish light of the 'cave', the four cousins found they were shivering as if it were all real. It was quite easy to play their parts after all! Anne actually felt genuinely excited when George – following the script based on the real story – gave her own special whistle to call Timmy to the rescue. The dog was shut up in a little room next to the studio. One of the camera crew opened the door, and Timmy bounded in ...

Everyone in the studio roared with laughter!

'Cut!' shouted Ralph Morris, furious. 'Is he supposed to be the Hound of the Baskervilles, or what?'

Well, the 'hound' was certainly Timmy – but what a state he was in! Left to himself, and feeling rather cross with his little mistress for deserting him, he had been passing the time by rummaging round the room where he was shut up. And he had tipped over some shelves with paint-pots standing on them. The paint had spilled all over him – so that was why poor Timmy looked so odd. He had green spots on one side of him and red stripes on the other side, while his head was a beautiful yellow and his tail was sky-blue! His own coat showed through the paint here and there, in reddish-brown patches. He did look funny!

They had to stop filming until Timmy had been cleaned up with turpentine. Not a very good start to his acting career – but after this unexpected hitch, the shooting of the film went along nicely, and Ralph was in a good temper again.

'Well done, children!' he told them at the end of the day. 'You all deserve congratulations!'

At that moment a complete stranger walked boldly in through the studio door and right on to the set.

He gave everyone a big grin. 'Hi, folks! You don't know me, but my name is Gary Findler!' he announced in a loud voice.

The children, the television actors and the technicians all stared at him wide-eyed. Gary Findler! Why, everyone had heard of *him*! He was an American multi-millionaire who had made a fortune from plastics, and his magnificent yacht was anchored in Southbourne harbour at this moment. The whole town was talking about him, and his picture had been in all the papers.

The American was a tall man with a shock of short grey hair. He was smiling broadly at everyone.

Dick nudged George. 'I say!' he whispered jokingly. 'The plastics king in person! Aren't we honoured!'

However, Ralph was frowning! 'The general

public isn't allowed into these studios, sir,' he said coldly.

'Well, I'm real sorry to intrude – but I was just so keen to meet you! Say – you *are* Mr Ralph Morris, aren't you?'

'Yes, that's me,' Ralph said. 'Er – what do you want?'

'Well, sir, I'm so interested in television, I'd just like to tell Miss Marshall and Mr Vane and all your wonderful team here how much I admire their work – and yours too as a director!'

Ralph felt rather flattered. 'You've come along at a good moment, really,' he said. 'We've just finished work for the time being, and everyone's here.'

He made the introductions all round, not forgetting the Five. Gary Findler seemed delighted to meet them.

'I certainly am in luck, finding you all here!' he said. 'Now I wonder – could I ask a great favour?'

Ralph looked at him a bit suspiciously. These millionaires – they thought they could do anything they liked! But his face soon cleared when he heard what the 'favour' was.

'I'm giving a party on board my yacht tomorrow evening,' the American explained. 'She's called the *Lucy Mae*, and she's lying in harbour here. Now, I was wondering if you'd be good enough to come along and join the party – all of you, and that includes the dog!' he added, smiling at the children.

The actors all accepted. George telephoned Uncle Quentin straight away. At first he was a little reluctant to say the children could go to the party, but in the end he agreed.

'That's fine, then,' said Ralph Morris. 'We'll be happy to come to your party tomorrow. And now let me show you round the studios.'

The next day was a very busy one for the children. They reached the studios early, so as to get plenty of filming done. The work went well – it was such fun that it was really more like play than work!

By now the professional actors were great friends with the children. They all stopped work on the film at about six o'clock, and the Five hurried back to the Rose Hotel to have their supper and get ready for the party on board the *Lucy Mae*.

Anne, who was just a little vain of her appearance and loved dressing up in pretty clothes, was chattering away excitedly. George didn't seem as keen on the party as you might have expected – the fact was, she was such a tomboy that she didn't like having to change out of her usual sweater and jeans and put on a dress instead! However, she knew she couldn't be the odd one out at such an elegant party.

Ralph Morris very kindly came to pick them up in his car. As soon as he turned into the parking place down by the harbour, the children let out cries of delight. The millionaire's yacht was ablaze with lights and coloured lanterns – even the gangplank had lights all along it. They could hear the faint sound of a band playing music. Goodness, what a party this was going to be!

Chapter Three

STEVE DISAPPEARS

Gary Findler was welcoming his guests on the deck, smiling broadly. Many of the important people of Southbourne were already there.

The American greeted the Five and Ralph warmly. 'So you kept your promise!' he said. 'Gee – it was real good of you to come!'

Steve and Suzy arrived together five minutes later. Steve's cousin, Mark, and the other actors soon arrived too – and now the party was in full swing. The yacht's big saloons, decorated in white and gold, were crammed with people.

Dick, who liked his food, decided that the well-stocked buffet table was the high spot of the evening! There were chicken patties, salmon sandwiches, jellies and ice-cream and all sorts of other delicious things. Timmy, a bit bewildered by the crowd, had decided to stay up on deck – along with an enormous bone which the kind ship's cook had found him.

In the biggest of the saloons, several couples were dancing. George, Julian and Anne enjoyed watching them whirl round and round. Everyone was having a grand time! But at last, at about one o'clock in the morning, Anne decided she'd been there long enough.

'I'm beginning to feel sleepy, George,' she confessed to her cousin. 'Suppose we go home now?'

'We'd better wait a little longer,' said George. 'Ralph promised to give us a lift back, but he doesn't seem to have noticed how late it is. We can't leave without him.'

However, the party was coming to an end. One by one, the guests said goodbye to their host, and soon the only people left were Ralph, the Five, and Suzy Marshall.

'Would you like a lift too, Suzy?' Ralph asked.

'No thank you, I'm waiting for Steve. He's supposed to be driving me back to my hotel – but I'm beginning to wonder where he is! He went off over an hour ago and said he'd be "back in a moment" – those were his very words. If you ask me, it's rather odd. I haven't seen him since, and I don't mind admitting I'm a bit worried.'

'Perhaps he didn't feel well?' said Ralph. 'I'll just go and look in the bathrooms.'

Following Gary Findler's directions, he went off to look, but he found no trace of Steve.

'No, he isn't there,' said Ralph when he came back.

Suzy looked alarmed. 'Then where can he be?'

That was the question they were all asking.

'Are you sure he didn't leave the boat?' asked the American. He sounded concerned.

Suzy nodded. 'Yes, I'm positive,' she said. 'And

'Perhaps he didn't feel well?' said Ralph.

if you ask me, it wouldn't be at all like Steve to leave me alone like that! As I told you, he said he'd be back in a moment.'

'It's certainly odd,' Ralph agreed.

George jumped up. Timmy will help us! Isn't that Steve's scarf you're holding, Suzy?' she asked. 'Let Tim smell it.'

Timmy sniffed at the scarf, and then looked at George.

'Seek, Timmy!' she said. 'Seek!'

But this time poor Timmy wasn't able to pick up a scent as he usually did. There had been so many people on board the yacht that evening, all crowded together, and the women had been wearing perfume – it was too much to ask him to pick out one particular person's scent among so many. George and the others decided to go and look for Steve themselves.

The children and their new friends, with the crew of the yacht to help them, searched the whole place. But they still found no sign of the actor. He seemed to have literally vanished into thin air! No one had set eyes on him after he left the saloon where Suzy had been waiting for him. Though they didn't find him, Ralph refused to panic.

'Perhaps Steve just forgot and went ashore, not remembering he'd left Suzy here,' he suggested.

'No,' said Gary Findler, shaking his head. 'I've already telephoned his hotel and even the local hospital, and he's not there.'

'Well, then,' said Ralph Morris, 'I'm afraid

we'll have to call the police and report him missing.'

Worried, the four children and Suzy agreed that there was really nothing else to be done.

Even though they had been disturbed in the middle of the night, the police soon turned up once they had been called. Two inspectors hurried to the yacht. They were rather impressed to get an emergency call from someone as well known as Gary Findler!

Unfortunately, even a police search of the yacht produced no results. Steve Vane was nowhere to be found on board!

Ralph and the children took poor Suzy back to her hotel. She was in tears. Before they went to bed themselves, the children discussed the puzzling end of the party.

'The police won't start making proper inquiries until tomorrow,' said George. 'Oh, poor Suzy – I do hope nothing serious has happened to Steve!'

But George occasionally had intuitions, and now something seemed to tell her that she and her cousins were facing a mystery once again – a mystery which mattered all the more because they were friends with the people involved in the drama. If, of course, there *was* any drama . . .

Next day the police did make a great many inquiries, but their report was disappointing. The police officers working on the case hadn't discovered anything. Inspector Wood, who was in charge, said the most likely explanation was that the missing actor had staged a 'disappearance' to create publicity.

The other actors, Ralph and the children all protested loudly.

'You must be wrong!' Ralph told the inspector. 'Steve would never do a thing like that!'

'Ralph's quite right,' Suzy backed him up. 'Steve's far too well known to need that sort of publicity! And if you ask me, he'd never have wanted me to be so worried! He'd have let me into the secret.'

As the shooting of the film had begun, Ralph couldn't interrupt it now, so he carried on with another actor, who looked very much like Steve, taking his part. However, the cast of the film were feeling depressed, and they didn't act with much conviction. The children were very sorry to see their friend Suzy so upset. They persuaded her to move from the small hotel where she was staying and take a room at the Rose Hotel, so that she would have them near her and wouldn't be so lonely. Suzy agreed, and she moved to the Rose Hotel that evening.

'You know, Suzy,' George said, 'I think it might be a good idea if we started making inquiries into Steve's disappearance ourselves. My cousins and I are used to solving mysteries! Would you like to help us?'

'Oh yes, I'd love to!' cried Suzy. 'If anyone can find Steve, I'm sure it's you!'

So George told the young actress her plan. She thought they should go back to the *Lucy Mae*, question Gary Findler and the crew again – and search the ship for a second time.

Suzy was pleased to think of actually *doing* something to help find Steve! Aunt Fanny and Uncle Quentin weren't in for supper, because they had been invited out by one of Uncle Quentin's scientist friends, and after the meal Suzy and the children found a taxi and set off to go down to the harbour.

But they found a disappointment waiting for them. The multi-millionaire was giving another party – a very grand reception – and a sailor on duty at the foot of the gangplank wouldn't let anyone on board without a formal invitation card. Millionaires have to be careful.

Suzy went up to the sailor and smiled at him.

'Mr Findler knows us,' she explained. 'I'm Suzy Marshall, and I've been on board the yacht before. Would you tell Mr Findler I'm here, and I must talk to him at once?'

'Sorry, miss!' said the sailor. 'I'm not supposed to leave my post for any reason whatever.'

'Oh dear,' said Suzy. 'If you ask me, Mr Findler wouldn't mind at all if we –'

But George interrupted. She had just seen the tall figure of the American up on deck, and she began waving and shouting, 'Mr Findler! Mr Findler!'

Timmy joined in, barking loudly.

'Woof! Woof!'

The noise they made, rising above the sound of soft music being played by a dance band, attracted the millionaire's attention. He leaned over the rail just as the sailor, feeling annoyed, grabbed George's shoulder and shook her quite roughly.

'You just stop that row, my lad! Shouting to people like that – what's the big idea?'

George shook him off and grabbed Timmy who was about to leap at the sailor and defend her! What with her short hair and the jeans she always wore, as well as her tomboyish ways, it wasn't the first time she had been taken for a boy!

'Don't you touch me!' she cried. 'If you do, you'd better watch out for my dog!'

'Hey, what's going on?' asked Gary Findler.

The sailor looked up, but Suzy spoke before he could reply.

'Oh, Mr Findler, it's me! Suzy Marshall. I *must* speak to you – it's urgent. And the children are here too.'

The American didn't look very pleased. Obviously, this was not a good moment for a private conversation. Gary Findler's last guest had come on board, and he was about to go and join the party in the saloons.

However, after hesitating for a moment he said, 'Okay, come on up.' When he saw that the children were following the young actress, he added, 'No, not you kids! There are too many folk aboard already – I invited a lot of important business contacts from London. I can't have you here now!'

Suzy hurried up the gangplank, giving the downcast children an apologetic smile, and disappeared into the yacht after Gary Findler.

Chapter Four

A TELEPHONE CALL

'Well, honestly! *He's* not very friendly today, is he?' said Dick in an aggrieved tone. 'Doesn't seem to think much of us now!'

'No – if that's how he feels, he needn't have seemed so pleased to meet us before!' Julian agreed.

'He *wasn't* very nice,' said Anne. Her feelings were hurt – not just for herself, but for the others too.

George felt really angry, as she saw the opportunity of carrying out inquiries on the spot slip away. Would Suzy be able to manage on her own? George was rather afraid not. But there was nothing she herself could do except wait, under the sailor's mocking eye.

Time seemed to be dragging, and the children began to feel restless. Dick said impatiently, 'What on earth can Suzy be doing? Surely it's time she was back?'

'If she's still on the yacht, I expect it's because she's managed to get some information out of

Gary Findler,' said Julian, sensible as ever.

'Hm,' said George. She wasn't so sure. 'I think Suzy's too excitable to be able to do that kind of thing very well. I just wish –'

But she was interrupted by the sight of another sailor coming down the gangplank. The man looked round, spotted the children and came over to them.

'Are you the kids they call the Famous Five?' he asked.

'Yes,' said Dick. 'What do you want?'

'There's a message for you from Miss Marshall. She says don't wait for her – go back to your hotel and she'll see you later. And she asked me to give you this for your taxi fare.'

The sailor handed Julian some money and went off again, leaving the children puzzled.

'So it looks as if Suzy will be there for some time, said Julian. He sighed. 'Oh, well, let's go back and go to bed!'

'Honestly! I'm disappointed in Suzy!' said George. 'She could have *insisted* on Gary Findler's asking us to come on board too!'

'Perhaps he invited her to join the party and she thought she'd liked to stay?' Anne suggested.

'Oh, Anne, you don't really think she'd feel like going to parties when Steve's just disappeared, do you?'

Anne went red.

'Look here,' said Dick, 'it's no use standing around on this quay arguing. That won't get us anywhere. Let's go back to the hotel!'

It was not really very late yet, so once they were

back at the Rose Hotel the children decided to stay up till Suzy came in. They were longing to know what she had managed to find out from Gary Findler. Perhaps the American had remembered some small detail which would help them to start along the right track?

They sat in George and Anne's room for about an hour, playing Snap. At least, Anne had an opportunity to use the tea-making equipment. Then the telephone in the room rang.

George jumped to her feet and picked up the receiver. 'Hallo?' she said.

She heard the hotel night porter's voice.

'Is that you, Miss Kirrin? I've got a call here for you from Miss Marshall.'

'It's Suzy!' George quickly told the others. 'Hallo, Suzy,' she said, as their friend came on the line. 'What happpened? Did you find out anything new? No? Nothing at all? Oh, what bad luck!'

She was repeating what Suzy said at the other end of the line, so that Julian, Dick and Anne would know what Suzy was telling them too.

'You say you're calling from a café?' she went on. 'Yes, I see – you thought we might be getting impatient to hear from you, and you're right, we weren't going to bed till you came in. We're waiting up for you, so do hurry up ... Oh, you mean you're telephoning to say you may not be back for quite a long time? But why not, Suzy? You want to go to the police station first? What? What did you say?'

There was a long silence. George was listening

hard, but she had stopped making comments. Her cousins waited in suspense. At last, George replaced the receiver.

'Suzy hung up, quite suddenly,' she told the others. She sounded puzzled. 'But first she told me she thinks she's being followed. She took a taxi from the harbour, and she saw a car with two men in it coming after her. So she stopped at the café, leaving the taxi waiting for her outside, and now she's going straight to the police station to try and get the two men in the car picked up. They could be the people who kidnapped Steve. If so, they·may want to get in touch with *her* and ask for a ransom – well, anyway, that's what Suzy thinks!'

Julian let out a whistle of surprise. 'Whew! The plot does seem to be thickening!'

'Yes, and if you ask me, Suzy's showing more initiative than I'd have expected, too!' said George thoughtfully.

'I bet those two men in the car are crooks,' said Dick.

Anne uttered a cry of alarm. 'Oh, my goodness! I do hope nothing happens to Suzy!'

George was looking cross. 'If you ask me, we can only wait – *and,* if you ask me, there's nothing worse than sitting about waiting!'

'Just listen to you!' said Dick, laughing. 'You've caught it from Suzy! Now *you're* starting everything with "If you ask me ..."!'

Instead of snapping at Dick for teasing her, George opened her mouth and closed it again, and then frowned. She seemed to be thinking hard.

'What shall we do now?' Anne asked her timidly.

'Anything you like!' said George, giving herself a little shake. 'Personally, I'm going down to the hall and I'm staying there till Suzy gets back.'

Naturally Julian, Dick, Anne and Timmy followed her down to the ground floor too. Sitting in the comfortable, deep armchairs in the hall of the hotel, the children soon began to doze off – and that was where Aunt Fanny and Uncle Quentin found them when they came in two hours later. George's father woke them up. He was rather cross.

It was after midnight, the children learned – and Suzy still wasn't back! Feeling alarmed, George told her parents what had been happening.

'What do *you* think, Uncle Quentin?' asked Julian. He was worried.

'I'll telephone the police station at once,' said Uncle Quentin, going into the public telephone box in the hall. 'They'll be able to give us news of Miss Marshall there.'

But they couldn't! The young actress had never been to the police station at all – no one there had seen her, all through the evening. The children had to accept the fact that Suzy too seemed to have disappeared! In between now and the time when she phoned the children to tell them she was going to the police, she had apparently vanished into thin air!

'That's ridiculous!' said Uncle Quentin. 'She must have been delayed somewhere.'

'Unless,' said George, looking rather pale, 'unless the crooks following her in that car captured her. I bet they were the people who kidnapped Steve!'

Suzy did not get back that night, or next morning either. Of course, once the police were informed of her disappearance, they started looking for her at once. They were still looking for Steve, too. Ralph Morris was very upset, but he still had to stick to his schedule for making the film, so he carried on with shooting. However, he said he wouldn't get a replacement for Suzy just yet.

'I'm sure they'll find her,' said Ralph hopefully. 'They *must* find her soon!'

But he was wrong. The day passed, and there was still no sign of Suzy. What's more, the policemen looking for the taxi the actress had taken the night before couldn't manage to track that down either. In spite of appeals on the local radio and in the *Southbourne Evening Star,* no taxi driver came forward to make a statement which would have helped the police.

Julian, Dick, Anne and George sat talking together at the end of the morning's shooting. They were all downcast.

'I'm sure Suzy's been kidnapped,' said George.

'But why?' asked Anne.

'For ransom, of course!' said Dick.

'But no one's asked a ransom for Steve yet,' Julian pointed out. 'And if Suzy's been kidnapped by the same people –'

'Do you know what I think?' said George. 'I believe Steve's kidnappers thought Suzy had found some kind of trail leading to them – and they kidnapped *her* to stop her talking! That's only a theory, but I like it. Well – isn't it time we made some more inquiries of our own?'

Chapter Five

WHAT HAS HAPPENED TO SUZY?

Later that afternoon the children had to go to the police station. Inspector Wood, the kindly officer in charge of the case, wanted them to sign the statements they had made. George, who liked the inspector, seized this chance to ask him some questions.

'We are awfully fond of Miss Marshall,' she said. 'We hate to think something might have happened to her! Except for the taxi driver who can't be traced, Mr Findler is the last person to have seen her. Do you mind telling us if he mentioned seeing any suspicious-looking car on the quayside when he said goodbye to Suzy?'

Inspector Wood smiled. He knew of the Five's reputation for being adventurous, and he had a strong notion that George was setting off on a private investigation of her own. Well, he didn't mind obliging her and her cousins!

'As a matter of fact, Mr Findler came in earlier to make a statement,' the friendly inspector told them. And he went on to describe his interview

'As a matter of fact, Mr. Findler came in earlier to make a statement,' the friendly Inspector told them.

with the multi-millionaire. Apparently Gary Findler had come to the police station of his own accord.

'Say, I'm real sorry to hear what happened to Miss Marshall!' he had said. 'I heard it on the radio. That poor kid! Yes, sure, she came to see me on board my yacht yesterday evening, along with those young friends of hers, the ones they call the Five. Well, I couldn't ask them all aboard right then – the place was crammed full with my guests from London – so I had a private chat with Miss Marshall in my study. She wanted me to search my memory for any kind of detail that might throw light on her fiancé's disappearance. I guess you know about him – the actor, Steve Vane. Well, it's just too bad, but I couldn't remember a thing, aside from Mr Vane leaving the saloon after he had a word with Miss Marshall, and that's all! I never saw him after that.'

'Did Miss Marshall spend long on your yacht yesterday evening, sir?'

'She certainly did, Inspector! To be frank with you, it was pretty inconvenient – I had my guests to look after, you see. Still, I felt sorry for the poor girl. She was real nervous and upset! I didn't have anything new to tell her, so I couldn't help, but I just said what I could to cheer her up – telling her I was sure the police would soon find her fiancé, that kind of thing. Then I went back up on deck with her, found her a passing taxi – no, I never saw any suspicious vehicle at all. Though I have to admit I was in a hurry to get back to my guests, so maybe I wasn't looking very closely.'

So Gary Findler's statement added nothing new to the few facts that were all the police had to go on. Feeling very glum, the children set off back to the studios. There was one more scene to be shot that day, involving Mark Turner and Timmy. Once the film was 'in the can', as the television people put it, the Five went down to the beach to stretch their legs – or in Timmy's case his paws.

'What are you thinking about, George?' Dick asked suddenly.

'Well, there's something bothering me – two things, in fact. First, why doesn't the driver of Suzy's taxi go to the police? There are so many appeals going out, he must know they want to talk to him – and he could be a great help!'

'Perhaps *he's* been kidnapped too?' suggested Anne.

'If so, we'd have heard about it. Someone would have reported a taxi driver missing. So I think it's odd he's keeping so quiet. But that's not what bothers me most,' George went on.

Her cousins were hanging on every word she said. 'Well, what is?' asked Julian. 'Come on, old thing, tell us!'

'All right! When I hung up after that phone conversation with Suzy, I found I kept saying "If you ask me!' *You* noticed that, Dick. Why? Well, because I was imitating Suzy. While we were talking, Suzy began more or less everything she said with those words!'

'I don't follow you,' said Dick, puzzled. 'We all know that's one of Suzy's habits!'

'Well, yes – she often *does* say, "If you ask me!"
But yesterday evening almost *everything* she said
began like that!'

'Surely that's not so surprising? She was in a
very excited state of mind.'

'Excited, yes – but if you're excited you
stammer, you get confused and fall over your own
words – you don't take extra special care to
emphasise a particular habit of yours, as Suzy was
doing!'

It was Julian's turn to look puzzled. 'What are
you getting at, George?'

'I heard her say "If you ask me" rather too many
times for my liking. It was intentional – she was
doing it on purpose!'

'But why would Suzy do a thing like that?'

'Exactly!' said George. 'I'm wondering if it
really *was* Suzy after all!'

There was a chorus of exclamations from the
others.

'What?' cried Dick. 'You mean to say –'

'*And,*' George went on, taking no notice of the
interruption, 'now that I come to think of it, I'm
not sure I recognised Suzy's voice!'

Several people had come nearer to the cousins,
so George led the others to the promenade. They
found an empty seat standing on its own, where
they wouldn't be overheard.

'You see,' she explained, 'I assumed straight
away it was Suzy, because the porter said so. And
then there was a woman's voice, sounding
slightly breathless saying, "Hallo, it's me –
Suzy!" So at the time I naturally thought it *was*

12

Suzy. I mean, there wasn't any *reason* to be suspicious! But now I think of it – no, I'm sure it wasn't Suzy's voice. It was a bit *like* her voice, but it wasn't the same.'

Feeling rather breathless herself, Anne asked, 'Do – do you mean somone was pretending to be Suzy? Trying to trick us?'

'That's what it looks like,' said George gloomily. 'I'm pretty sure the crooks had already kidnapped Suzy when we got that phone call. I expect the taxi Mr Findler saw wasn't a real taxi at all – it was driven by one of the crooks. That would explain everything!'

Dick jumped up from the seat and faced his cousin. 'Crooks?' he said. 'But *what* crooks, for goodness sake, George?'

'Woof!' said Timmy, as if he wanted to join in the conversation too.

'Yes, what crooks?' Julian repeated. He sighed. 'We don't know anything about them. We haven't got a single clue to help us. You know, we've never started investigating a mystery with less chance of solving it before!'

'Oh, never mind that!' cried George. *She* didn't care about difficulties – they were only a challenge to her! 'I'm sure we shall manage to solve this mystery too – even though it's a double one. We'll find Steve and Suzy. If we can't – well, the Five had better go into retirement!'

'Oh, we can't do that.' said Dick.

'Let's go over everything carefully,' said Julian. 'You tell us what you think happened, George.'

'Well, this is what I think,' George told them. 'The crooks must have been watching Suzy. They followed us down to the harbour, and waited for her to come off the yacht again. We made things easier for them by going back to the hotel. I ought not to have been so trusting! When Suzy did come back to the quay, it was easy for them to get her into a fake taxi. If we'd stayed I expect they might still have found some way to dispose of us and then kidnap Suzy – but in any case, she's in their hands now, along with Steve!'

It was only too clear, the children thought.

Julian, who respected George's quick mind, asked her advice. 'What do you think we ought to do about it, George?'

'List all the possible suspects and keep a close watch on them,' said George at once.

And so the children spent the evening drawing up a list of people who might somehow or other be involved in the double disappearance of Steve and Suzy.

'I suppose the television people are our first suspects,' said Dick. 'They knew more about Steve and Suzy's comings and goings than anybody else.'

'Oh, don't be silly!' cried Anne indignantly. 'How *can* you think Ralph or Mark or any of the others would be guilty of a thing like that? After all, Mark is Steve's cousin.'

'I didn't say I thought anyone was guilty,' replied Dick. 'But we can't rule people out straight away just because we happen to like them.'

'Dick's right,' George put in. 'We'll do it by a process of elimination! Tomorrow we'll start observing all our suspects carefully. Only we mustn't let them see us doing it! Maybe we'll find some clue ...'

*   *   *

Next day the cast of the film were back in front of the cameras again. The children's list of suspects began with Ralph Morris, Mark Turner, John Ferris and Emlyn Jones. Then, of course, there were the cameramen and technicians working on the film. And the children added the mysterious Mr X and Mr Y who had been driving a car or cars on the night of Suzy's disappearance, and who might have kidnapped Steve and Suzy for ransom.

'Let's concentrate on Ralph and the actors for a start,' George decided.

Well, it was easy enough to eliminate Ralph! The success of his film depended on the two stars who had disappeared, as well as the Five, so he wouldn't be doing himself much good by getting Steve and Suzy out of the way. The children all liked Ralph, and they could see he was really upset. It was impossible to imagine him hatching a plot against the young actor and actress.

Mark was not playing his part with much enthusiasm today. His nerves were obviously stretched to breaking point.

'Which could show that he has a guilty

conscience,' suggested Dick.

John Ferris, a rather jolly, stoutish man, usually always ready to crack a joke, seemed badly upset by Steve and Suzy's disappearance as well.

'Almost *too* badly upset,' remarked Julian thoughtfully. 'He's piling it on a bit thick! Such a complete change of character from one day to the next – and remember, he *is* an actor.'

'Do you really think he's just pretending?' asked Anne in dismay. 'Oh no! I just can't believe any of them could be in league with the kidnappers!'

'Personally, I think Emlyn Jones is behaving rather oddly,' said George. 'It struck me before that he seems to be a little jealous of Steve's success. And unlike the others, *he* doesn't seem particularly upset now that Steve's vanished!'

All day, while they went on working under the bright studio lights, the four cousins were watching their fellow actors. There were all sorts of questions still to be answered – and they had a long way to go before they could hope to get an idea of who was really behind the disappearance of Steve and Suzy. But George for one was sure that persistence would pay off in the end!

Chapter Six

A NEW THEORY –
AND A NEW ACTRESS

At the end of that day's shooting, the children held another council. They wanted to take stock of their position.

'The more I think about it,' said George, 'the more I doubt whether the real culprit is working on our television film. None of the actors seems to have any good reason to kidnap Steve, and as for Suzy –'

George suddenly stopped, frowning.

'Yes?' inquired Julian. 'What were you going to say? As for Suzy – ?'

'As for Suzy – well, I've just realised that there *is* someone who could have easily kidnapped her! Only the person I'm thinking of seems to have even less motive for it than the rest of our suspects!'

'Who are you talking about?' asked Dick impatiently.

'Gary Findler, of course!'

'Gary Findler?' exclaimed Julian, Dick and Anne, in chorus.

'Why, yes! Look – it would have been so simple for him! Remember, Suzy went on board the *Lucy Mae* of her own free will! He only needed to keep her there, and get *us* out of the way by sending that sailor with a misleading message for us.'

'George, are you nuts?' protested Julian. 'Mr Findler didn't even know Steve or Suzy before he met them at the studio the other day!'

George looked her cousin straight in the eye. 'How do you know he didn't know them, Ju?' she replied. 'That's how it *seemed*, but there's nothing to prove it.'

'Well, Steve and Suzy certainly didn't know him!'

'No, you're right there – but do let me finish what I was saying! Suppose Gary Findler got rid of us by sending us back to the hotel, then the coast was clear for him. He wouldn't even have needed a fake taxi. He just had to keep Suzy there on board. And then, a little later, suppose he got a woman to phone us saying she was Suzy? As the crowning touch! How's that for a theory?'

Dick looked bewildered. 'But why make the phone call at all?'

'Because if she said she was being followed by a car, the person pretending to be Suzy would draw suspicion away from the yacht. Everyone would be bound to think that Suzy had been kidnapped *after* she left the *Lucy Mae*, not on the yacht itself.'

Dick looked doubtful. 'It's a bit far-fetched, you know! Why would Gary Findler act like that? He's so rich, he can hardly need to kidnap people for ransom as a way of getting money. So why do it?'

'I've no idea,' George admitted, sighing. 'All I'm saying is that it would have been easier for him than anyone else to kidnap Suzy!'

'And what about Steve? Honestly, George, I think you're right off the rails this time!'

But George stuck to her guns. She sometimes had what she called a 'funny feeling', and some of her funny feelings turned out to be right. Although sometimes her imagination did run away with her and let her in for a disappointment!

She certainly had a disappointment when, eager to share her suspicions with someone, she went to see friendly Inspector Wood. The Inspector listened to what George had to say, and then gave her an indulgent but amused smile.

'I'm afraid you're going rather too far this time,' he said in a kindly tone. 'And you know, it's a serious matter to make accusations against someone. You admit that you have no evidence to back up this theory of yours! You do realise the gravity of what you're saying, don't you?'

George went bright red. Her cousins, who were with her, felt sympathetic. 'But it's true,' thought Anne, 'George *does* sometimes exaggerate! I wish she'd listened to us and kept her suspicions to herself!'

As George did not reply, Inspector Wood went on, 'Besides, Mr Findler is a very well-known person, with a high reputation for honesty. He's above suspicion. It's sheer coincidence that his name is linked in any way with the disappearance of Miss Marshall.' Then, seeing how unhappy George looked, he added, 'Anyway, thank you for telling me about your idea, but I repeat, it has no foundation in fact, and you'd better not go spreading it in public. In my opinion, Miss Marshall and Mr Vane were kidnapped because someone hopes to demand a big ransom for them. We can't do anything but wait until the kidnappers show their hand.'

He rose to his feet, and George realised the conversation was over. She left the police station looking miserable. Her cousins, who knew how hot-tempered she could be, felt the wisest thing was not to say anything to her just now.

*   *   *

But time went by, and there was *still* no ransom demand for either Steve or Suzy.

Ralph Morris decided, regretfully, that he would have to find someone else for Suzy's part in the film, and he advertised for an actress to take her place. He needed someone who looked as much like Suzy as possible. And on the very day the advertisement appeared in the papers, a girl turned up at the studios. She had done some work in television before, and she was about Suzy's age and height. Her name was Isabel Dunn. Ralph gave Isabel a quick audition for the part, and then engaged her. He introduced her to the rest of the cast. The other actors were pleased to welcome the newcomer, especially as it meant work on the film could continue, but the children were not so sure about her. Perhaps that was because of Timmy's attitude. The dog took a dislike to Isabel from the very start. When she put out a hand to pat him, he growled, and his hair bristled.

'That's funny,' George told her cousins in an undertone. 'Tim's usually the friendliest of dogs! You know, I feel a bit suspicious of this Isabel!'

Julian, Dick and Anne laughed at her.

'My poor, dear old George,' Dick said, 'ever since our friends disappeared you've been seeing suspects everywhere! It's becoming an obsession!'

This time, however, George turned out to be right! For once during this adventure, luck was on the side of the children. They had been shooting an open-air sequence on the Downs outside Southbourne, and Ralph said it was time for a break. Pleased to have a chance to relax, the actors went strolling off into the countryside. The children were walking along a lane between high banks when they suddenly recognised Isabel's voice.

Peering through the hedge, they saw the actress standing by the side of the main road, deep in conversation with a young man at the wheel of a powerful sports car.

'Hallo,' said Julian, 'it looks as if she's met someone she knows.'

'He may just have stopped to ask her the way.' Anne suggested.

51

The dog took a dislike to Isabel from the very start.

Behind the hedge, the four cousins couldn't help hearing the words carried to them on the wind.

'I don't think that's it,' said George, suddenly very interested in the couple. 'They really *do* seem to know each other.'

'In fact, they know each other so well that he's busy telling Isabel off!' added Dick, laughing.

He was right. The man in the car certainly sounded angry as he talked to the young actress. Behind their hedge, the four cousins couldn't help hearing the words carried to them on the wind.

'What a crazy idea of yours; answering that advertisement for Suzy Marhsall's part! I told you it was idiotic at the time, and I still say so. Those kids might easily recognise your voice, and *then* we'd be in a nice mess! When the boss hears about this he'll be furious!'

'Oh, come on, Paul,' Isabel said. 'I'm an actress first and foremost, you know! I saw my chance and I took it. I don't see why the boss should mind.'

The man called Paul laughed. 'Oh, don't you, indeed?'

'No, I don't! And I'll tell you why – I'm one of the cast of the film now, which means I can be a lot more useful to him. What's more, if anyone's got a right to shout at me like that, it's him and not you!'

The driver of the car started it with a violent jerk, and disappeared round the next bend in the road. Isabel went on walking.

'Well, well!' murmured George. 'So *now* we know where we are!'

'What do you mean?' asked Anne.

'I mean that conversation explains everything! What do you say, Julian?'

Her tall, fair-haired cousin frowned.

'Yes, it certainly explains a lot,' he said. 'Isabel and that man Paul are obviously part of a gang. And equally obviously, they're plotting something which is to do with our television film.'

'*And* the disappearance of Steve and Suzy,' Dick added.

'What's more,' said George, 'Paul is afraid we may recognise Isabel's voice! So that means we've heard it before, in suspicious circumstances – such as?'

'Such as the time when the woman who said she was Suzy spoke to you on the phone!' Anne finished.

'Well done, Anne! We're on the trail at last!'

George was getting very excited. But sensible Julian brought her down to earth!

'Take it easy, George! You're forgetting one very important point. We have no idea who this "boss" Paul mentioned may be.'

'Oh, never mind – we've got a really good lead now! If we keep watch on Isabel, we'll be sure to find our way to the mysterious boss of this gang!' said George confidently.

Chapter Seven

AN ACCIDENT IN THE STUDIO!

Of course, the disappearance of first Steve and then Suzy had upset Ralph's plan for the order in which he was going to shoot the different scenes of the film. The day after the Five had happened to overhear that interesting conversation between Isabel and her friend Paul, he decided to shoot a sequence in the 'Smugglers' Cave' again. They were using a set which showed the cave made of plywood, cardboard and polystyrene – it looked very genuine. There were big wooden 'rocks' overhanging it, to make it even more like the real thing.

The scene began with the smugglers meeting in their cave. Mark, playing one of the gang, had to start a quarrel and then storm furiously out of the meeting.

Ralph told the actors what he wanted them to do. The Five stood in a group behind the camera, watching the same scene being shot and waiting for their turn to come on. Timmy, remembering his accident with the paint, was being very good.

'Right, Mark!' said Ralph. 'That last outburst of yours – deliver it in a snarling tone, then turn your back on the others and march out of the cave clenching your fists. Get the idea? Fine! Off you go, then. Shoot!'

Mark spoke his lines, turned on his heel and left the cave. The camera slowly moved backwards as he approached it.

What happened next was so sudden that it left everyone dazed. Just as Mark was emerging from the mouth of the cave, one of the huge fake rocks above the actor broke away from the scenery and fell on him!

Mark collapsed with a groan of pain. George and Ralph were the first to run to his aid.

'Are you hurt, Mark?' asked the director. He sounded very worried.

'I – I think it's my shoulder.'

Poor Mark was very pale indeed. His face was twisted with pain. Tender-hearted Anne bent over him.

'Let me help you off with your jacket,' she offered.

But any movement at all made the injured man cry out.

'We must call a doctor, quick!' said Ralph, in dismay.

One of the technicians rushed to the phone and the doctor soon came. He examined the injured shoulder and shook his head.

'It's dislocated,' he said. 'That's not too serious, but it can be inconvenient. There doesn't seem to be any injury to the bone itself, but we'll

Ralph told the actors what he wanted them to do.

One of the huge fake rocks above the actor broke away from the scenery and fell on him!

have to X-ray it to make sure. I'll call an ambulance.'

Poor Mark, although he was in considerable pain, was worrying about the future of the film and about being a nuisance to the others.

'What a stupid accident!' he said angrily. 'That really puts the lid on it! How will you manage now, Ralph?'

Ralph reassured his friend, and while he was talking to Mark the ambulance arrived. The ambulance men carefully lifted the patient and put him into the vehicle. 'Mark, would you like us to come with you?' Dick asked on the spur of the moment.

But Ralph Morris didn't give Mark a chance to reply.

'No, no,' he said. 'It's my job to go with Mark. I'll wait at the hospital for the result of the X-rays, and then we'll know where we are. Let's hope for the best! Meanwhile, the rest of you can be learning some of your lines.'

With these words, he got into the ambulance with Mark, and it started off. George and her cousins watched it drive away.

It was almost twelve o'clock, and the other actors suggested that the children might as well go back to their hotel for lunch. 'Come back to the studio early in the afternoon,' John Ferris told them. 'We should know how Mark's doing by then. Luckily the scene Ralph's planning to shoot this afternoon is one where he doesn't appear.'

The Five ate their lunch quickly. 'Are you

going straight back to the studio?' Uncle Quentin asked them.

'Yes, Father,' said George. 'We want to know if Mark's seriously hurt or not.'

And the children and Timmy hurried back to South-East Television Studios. Isabel, John and the others were there already.

'Well?' George asked. 'Where's Ralph? What did they say at the hospital?'

'We don't know,' said John Ferris. 'Ralph isn't even back yet.'

'But surely he phoned?' asked Dick.

'No, he hasn't phoned either – and he seemed to be in such a hurry when they left!'

'That's odd,' said George. 'Have *you* phoned the hospital?'

John Ferris's rather chubby face went red. 'Do you know, I never thought of that!' he confessed. 'I'll do it right away!'

Everyone gathered round him, eager to hear news of Mark. But no sooner did John get through to the hospital than an expression of dismay came over his face.

'What?' he exclaimed. 'You mean no ambulance brought in a patient called Mark Turner at all this morning? But that can't be true – we saw it leaving with our own eyes!'

There was silence, while John listened. Then he said, 'He's a television actor. And Ralph Morris, the well-known director, was with him. Yes please, would you check? We're all very worried here at the studios.'

Then there was another silence. George was

bursting with impatience.

'No, I'm afraid there is definitely no patient by the name of Mark Turner in the hospital. I'm sorry we can't help you.'

John hung up as the line went dead.

'Well!' he exclaimed, bewildered. 'This is really extraordinary! The ambulance that took Mark and Ralph away this morning can never have reached the hospital! I wonder –'

But they never knew what he wondered, because the telephone rang. George was the first to reach it and quickly lifted the receiver. Something told her this call was to do with their adventure – and she was right! It was Inspector Wood, ringing South-East Television.

'Oh, hallo, Inspector – this is George Kirrin speaking!'

'Well, you'll be the first to hear the news,' said the Inspector, 'and I'd be glad if you'd tell everyone else involved in that film of yours. Your director, Mr Morris, has been found, half stunned, in a quiet street between the studios and the town centre.'

'Good gracious!' cried George. 'Where is he now?'

'He asked us to take him to a private clinic run by a friend of his. I don't think he's badly hurt. He says you're not to worry, and he hopes he'll be back with you tomorrow morning.'

George was on tenterhooks. 'But what exactly happened to him?' she asked.

'He couldn't make a very long statement, considering the condition he was in. But he was accompanying the actor Mark Turner to hospital in an ambulance, when they were stopped by a black car which barred their way. The two men in the car knocked out the ambulance men and Mr Morris, and then put them out of the vehicle. That's all Mr Morris knows. As the ambulance has disappeared, it looks as if the criminals went off with it.'

'What about Mark?'

'He hasn't been found, so it seems likely that the men kidnapped him.'

'If they forced the ambulance to stop, I'm sure it was on purpose to kidnap Mark!' cried George.

'Well, we can't be certain of that – so don't go getting over-excited again, young lady!'

Inspector Wood hung up, leaving George decidedly annoyed, as much by being called 'young lady' as by the Inspector's news. She would have so liked to be a boy!

Meanwhile, the others were seething with impatience.

'Well, what did he tell you?' Julian asked.

George repeated her conversation with the Inspector. Everyone was very depressed – it really did look as if Fate was against them!

'Whose turn next, I wonder?' said Isabel quietly.

George shot her a quick glance. Just where had Isabel been at the moment when the wooden rock came adrift from the rest of the scenery? Could she have pushed it, to make it fall on Mark?

'Hold on!' George told herself. 'I mustn't get carried away again!'

*   *   *

Next day, Ralph Morris kept his word, and was back at South-East Television Studios. His head was bandaged, and he looked pale and drawn, but otherwise he was all right, and he was absolutely determined to carry on shooting the film, though he would have to use another actor instead of Mark now.

'I'd never have believed it possible,' he told the others. 'Imagine an ambulance being attacked almost in the middle of a busy town, and an injured man being abducted from it! Poor Mark! What on earth can these mysterious kidnappers have against him? First it was Steve, then Suzy, and now Mark's their third victim!'

'So you agree with us?' cried George. '*You* see a link between the three incidents too?'

'I certainly do! You know, if I thought I had any real enemies I'd even think the kidnappings were meant to hurt me personally! It's as if someone was determined to sabotage my film – and I just hope nothing will happen to you children.' And he looked at the children with a worried expression in his eyes.

But George and her cousins, who had discussed the whole situation at length the day before, didn't feel that they were in any danger. They had an idea it all turned on some mystery which was nothing to do with Ralph or his film.

'But it wouldn't be any use trying to explain that to grown-ups,' George had said, at the end of their discussion. 'They'd only say my imagination was working overtime again! You just wait, though – I bet I *shall* be proved right in the end!'

Chapter Eight

ALICE ARRIVES

However, while they did wait, they were no farther on than before! The children knew they had no solid evidence to back up any of their theories, and no clues to lead them anywhere.

About mid-day, two policemen came to the studios to ask Ralph Morris some more questions. Their interview with him was quite short. He hadn't remembered any other details, so he had nothing to add to what he had said before.

But the policemen did tell him and his actors one interesting piece of news: the ambulance had been found!

'It was abandoned by the roadside, not far from the sea. Some holidaymakers spotted it partly hidden behind some bushes, and they informed us at once.'

'What about Mark – I mean Mr Turner?' asked George anxiously.

'Mr Turner wasn't in it, and that confirms what you suspected – the men who stopped the ambulance did so on purpose to kidnap him!'

When the policemen had left, the actors sat down to have a picnic lunch in the studio. Ralph said he wasn't hungry.

'Oh, but you *must* eat!' Anne insisted, worried about their friend's health. 'After all you've been through, you really need something to keep your strength up!'

Ralph smiled. Anne, who was so thoughtful and sweet-natured, was his favourite among the children! To please her, he agreed to share the picnic they had brought from the hotel – the manageress had provided a really good packed lunch of cheese and egg sandwiches, tomatoes, and slabs of fruit cake to follow. Even Timmy looked as if he were encouraging the director to eat!

George was enjoying her lunch, but she couldn't stop thinking about the mystery of the kidnapping – a triple kidnapping now!

'If only we could find some link between our three friends, apart from the fact that they're all actors!' she sighed. 'But I just can't see any connection!'

'And there *isn't* any connection,' Ralph agreed gloomily.

'Wait a minute,' said Julian. 'What about the fact that Mark and Steve are cousins?'

'Oh, yes, I'd forgotten that,' said George.

'How can they be cousins?' asked Anne, 'They don't have the same surname, like George and all of us do.'

'Well, with us, it's our fathers who are brothers,' explained Julian, 'but I expect that

Mark's mother and Steve's mother are sisters, so they would have different surnames.'

Ralph nodded.

Dick was impatient at these explanations. He looked at George to see if she thought this was an important clue.

'What do you think, George?' he asked. 'Do you think it matters?'

'Yes,' said George at once, her face red with excitement, 'that would link them all together. It certainly could be important – well, anyway, it's something to think about.

'As if we hadn't done enough thinking already!' groaned Dick, making a face.

George frowned. 'You never know what piece of information may come in useful!' she told him. 'The thing is to decide which bits really aren't any help, and discard them, while you hang on to the ones that *are* useful.'

'Oh dear!' sighed Anne. 'Sorting them out isn't always easy!'

'Woof!' said Timmy, who thought it was about time someone paid *him* some attention.

'Well,' said George, 'let's count up the facts we have so far. Our three kidnapped friends are all more or less related. Steve and Mark are cousins – and Suzy is engaged to Steve and they're going to get married quite soon. Those are facts, and we musn't lose sight of them!'

*   *   *

That day, the cast of the film worked hard, but

without much enthusiasm. Mark's disappearance was weighing on everyone's mind. Late in the afternoon, Ralph Morris had a phone call from London. Mark's wife Alice, who was badly upset by the kidnapping of her husband, said she was going to come to Southbourne the next day. She wanted to be on the spot while the police made their inquiries, and see the scene of the drama for herself.

'I hope having her here won't mean any more complications!' said George.

The children said they would go with Ralph when he went to the station to meet Mark's wife. They all liked Alice Turner straight away. She was a small, slim young woman with pretty dark hair, and a sad smile which went straight to Anne's tender heart.

George, Dick and Julian all swore to themselves to find her husband for her, and Tim licked her hand and wagged his tail.

'Oh, how kind of you all to come and meet me!' said Alice, when she had been introduced all round. Then she sighed. 'I suppose there isn't anything new to tell me? Have they found any trace of Mark yet?' Her eyes filled with tears.

Talking to the police took up most of Alice's morning, but then she had lunch with the actors and the production team in a little café near the studios. The children, who felt very sorry for her, chatted to her as if she were an old friend. George, with the mystery of the kidnappings in mind, bombarded her with questions, but there was very little Alice could tell her.

'Good gracious, no!' said Alice. 'My husband hasn't got an enemy in the world! And the same is true of Steve – everyone likes them, and they're both very easy to get on with.'

The cast of the film were soon firm friends with Alice. She decided to stay on in Southbourne until Mark was found. The police were busy working on the case – though, it must be admitted, without getting anything much in the way of results. As for the Five, they too seemed to be marking time.

Ralph, who was really upset to see Alice so sad had a good idea. He gave her a part as an extra in the film. That meant she had something to do, as well as the chance of earning a little money. She eagerly accepted his offer – she was glad of anything that would take her mind off her troubles.

'You're all so good to me,' the young woman told the children. 'It gives me courage, if not hope.'

'Oh, you mustn't give up hope,' Julian said earnestly. 'Mark is a good friend of ours, and we've sworn to find him!'

Timmy went up to Alice and solemnly offered to shake paws with her, as if he wanted to make a contribution too!

'There, look!' said George cheerfully. 'My dog's promising to help you as well!'

'I'm sure your husband can't be in real danger,' Dick added. 'The mystery will be cleared up sooner or later, and then Mark and Steve and Suzy will all be back.'

'Let's hope it won't be *too* much later!' sighed Alice, but she smiled bravely.

The children didn't know just what they could do to cheer their new friend up. In between shooting scenes of the film, they sometimes took her swimming with them. At other times they hired a rowing boat and went out on the sea. One afternoon, Ralph decided to film a scene against a background of real rocks at a place called Cormorant's Cape. George and her cousins said they wouldn't go there by road, like everyone else, but would take Alice and go by sea – it would be a nice outing for their friend.

George was very good at handling all sorts of boats – she had her own rowing boat at Kirrin Cottage, and was always rowing out to her very own Kirrin Island in it. She had spent a lot of time out at sea in all kinds of weather. Alice didn't hesitate to accept when Julian asked her if she would like to join the expedition to Cormorant's Cape. She really enjoyed the trip, and didn't feel quite as worried as usual, as the children's friendly chatter helped to take her mind off her missing husband for a while. She knew she could trust the children, and thought that if anyone was going to find her husband, they would do it.

George steered the boat out of Southbourne harbour and round the headland to Cormorant's Cape. Julian and Dick each took a pair of oars and rowed. They arrived at the spot where they were to meet Ralph Morris at just the right time.

'Good – there you are!' cried Ralph, seeing Alice and the children. 'Come on – the camera's ready, and so is the audience!' he added, pointing to several holiday-makers who were hanging around to watch. 'Let's get started!'

It was quite hard work filming the scene, because the sun was blazing down, and Ralph worked his actors hard, scarcely allowing them a moment's rest. At last he said they could have a break, and everyone heaved a sigh of relief.

'You can have three-quarters of an hour,' Ralph told them. 'After that we'll all start again. We want to get this scene in the can today!'

Let's make the most of this break,' said Julian. 'I vote we swim! It would do us good and we've brought our swimming things.'

'Oh yes, let's bathe!' George agreed. 'Come on everyone – back on board the boat! Somebody told me there's a quiet little bay around the next headland. It's difficult to get there except by sea, so you don't often find many people on the beach.'

Sure enough, the spot was deserted. It would be fun to swim there all on their own! George, her cousins and Alice clambered out of the boat. This part of the coast was quite wild, with a sandy beach and rocks beyond it. In a moment the children and Alice were enjoying splashing about in the water. Timmy thought it was lovely too. He was a good swimmer, strong and powerful.

Alice wasn't quite such a strong swimmer as the children, and they thoughtfully slowed down to her pace, so that she would feel at ease. Then they had a game of ball – Timmy really shone at

Julian and Dick each took a pair of oars and rowed.

In a moment the children and Alice were enjoying splashing about in the water.

that! By then it was time to think of getting back.

Alice's bathing suit wasn't quite dry, and she quickly disappeared behind a large rock.

'I won't be a minute!' she called to the children. 'I'll change as quickly as I can.'

George and her cousins lay basking in the sun as they waited for Alice, their eyes closed so as not to be dazzled.

Suddenly Dick started laughing. 'Honestly – women are all the same!' he said. 'They take *ages* getting dressed. Alice's "minute" is more like ten!'

'You're right!' said Julian, sitting up with a start. 'And Ralph won't like it if we're late.'

'Oh dear – I hope nothing's happened to Alice!' said Anne, immediately feeling worried.

George thumped her cousin on the back. 'Well, don't just sit there wondering about it!' she said. 'Try calling!'

And cupping her own hands round her mouth, she shouted towards the big rock behind which Alice had disappeared.

'Hey – Alice! Hurry up! We've got to leave.'

There was no reply but a faint echo. Julian tried.

'*Alice*!' he shouted. 'Alice, hurry up!'

'Oh dear!' said Anne. 'She isn't replying – I'm afraid something *has* happened to her.'

'Perhaps she doesn't feel well?' suggested Dick. He wasn't laughing now. 'The sun's so hot today!'

'Well let's go and see,' said George sensibly.

And she started off towards the big rock,

without stopping to see whether the others were following her. When her cousins caught up, they found her standing rooted to the spot, staring at something lying on the sand rolled up in a ball.

It was Alice's bathing suit. But Alice herself wasn't there any more. She and her clothes had simply disappeared! Just like Steve, Suzy and Mark!

Chapter Nine

A FOURTH DISAPPEARANCE

'Oh no – it just isn't possible!' stammered George in dismay. 'She was *here*, quite close to us! She's vanished almost before our eyes.'

In fact this upset her more than anything. Mark's wife had apparently dissolved into thin air while she was, in a way, the responsibility of the Five.

'First Suzy and Steve, now Alice and Mark,' said Julian.

'No!' repeated George. 'It just isn't possible – it *can't* be possible!'

But there was nothing she could do in the face of the evidence, and though the children searched the beach of the little bay, and the rocks beyond, and Timmy sniffed all round the place, they didn't find any sign of Alice. She really did seem to have vanished.

When poor Ralph heard the news, he looked quite ill. John Ferris, who was in the scene they'd been shooting, was stunned too. However, George didn't give them time to stand about wondering how it had happened.

'Come on, *quick*!' she begged. 'There's not a moment to lose! We must telephone Inspector Wood and ask him to come here at once.'

What an uproar there was! Inspector Wood went right off the deep end! He felt that his own reputation was at stake. Ever since Steve's disappearance – the first of the four – his inquiries had got nowhere at all. The mysterious kidnappers were going off with their victims under his very nose, and he was furious!

George was furious too. While the police went carefully over the beach where Alice had last been seen with a fine toothcomb, the Inspector questioned the children, who were the only witnesses of her disappearance. Not that they could really be called *witnesses*, since they hadn't seen or heard anything at all!

'It was all so sudden,' Julian explained. As usual, he managed to stay calm and collected. 'We were lying on the beach waiting for Alice, and it certainly didn't look as if there was anyone else about. I just can't understand it.'

In fact, nobody could understand it!

'And this time,' grunted Inspector Wood, 'we can't even think of it as a put-up job, like that business with the ambulance! No one could have known Mrs Turner was going to swim in that lonely bay – no one but you children, that is.'

'My goodness!' muttered George, trying not to lose her temper. 'Any moment now he'll be suspecting *us*!'

Late that afternoon they all gathered together

for a discussion in the boys' room at the Rose Hotel. The door to the balcony stood open, and the sun shone in, still quite warm.

George was seething with impatience. 'We must *do* something!' she said.

'I vote we go in for a spot of kidnapping ourselves!' suggested Dick boldly. 'Why don't we kidnap Isabel, shut her up somewhere and make her talk?'

'Oh, don't be more of an idiot than you can help!' Julian told his brother. 'Keep Isabel shut up *where*? And *how* would we make her talk? No, what we need is some clue to this latest disappearance – something to link Alice to Steve, Suzy and Mark.'

'But we haven't *got* a clue,' said Anne miserably. 'There wasn't a soul on the beach but us!'

'How do you know?' said George. 'Someone could have come ashore a little way off, in another bay, come up behind us by land and taken Alice by surprise. After all, the rocks cut off our view of the country inland. And we had our eyes shut while we were sunbathing, too.'

'Alice would have screamed!' Dick protested.

'Not if it was a surprise attack, and they'd gagged her at once.'

'Listen, everyone!' said Julian. He was obviously thinking very carefully about what he was saying. 'There's something I ought to tell you. I didn't mention it before, because I wanted time to think it over – and I didn't want to do anything rashly. Giving false evidence is a very serious matter! And then – well, George, I *was* a bit afraid of your imagination running away with you again – you know you *are* rather apt to –'

'Oh, stop it!' growled George. 'Do come to the point, Ju! If you've got anything to say go ahead and say it! We're all listening.'

Dick and Anne were eager to hear what Julian had to say too, and he launched into his story.

'I don't know if what I saw had any connection with the kidnapping of Alice – if it really *was* a kidnapping,' he added cautiously. 'But while we were bathing, I saw –'

He stopped again. George nearly blew up then and there!

'Are you *ever* coming to the point? You and your ifs and buts! *What* did you see?'

'Gary Findler's yacht – the *Lucy Mae*! She was cruising a little way out to sea, at a very low speed.'

'Gosh!' gasped Dick.

George's eyes began to shine. However, she made herself ask calmly, 'Are you sure? I didn't see anything myself. I'm sure I would have noticed the yacht.'

'You were playing ball with Dick and Timmy at the time. You just didn't happen to be looking that way, that's all.'

'And I saw the yacht too!' said Anne in her clear little voice. 'Ju's right. I recognised it at once, But I didn't think of mentioning it to anyone.'

Anne's evidence backed up Julian's story. So while Alice and the Five were splashing about in the water, the American's yacht had been passing not far away! Gary Findler himself or someone else aboard the yacht, using field glasses, could easily have made out the faces of the children and their companion. In which case . . .

George felt her suspicions revive again. Her instinctive distrust of Gary Findler was stronger than ever now. She knew Inspector Wood had only laughed at her when she told him what she suspected – but perhaps the Inspector had been wrong to laugh!

'Listen!' she said urgently. 'I'm sure we've got a good clue now – that yacht turning up just when Alice happened to be with us. You can laugh at my vivid imagination if you like, Ju, but I'm more certain than ever there's a link between Gary Findler and Steve, Suzy, Mark and Alice.'

'But what sort of link?' asked Dick.

'If we knew that there wouldn't be any mystery, would there? We're still in the dark! But all the same, I can see a glimmer of light ahead.'

'There hasn't been a single ransom demand yet,' Julian reminded her.

'I know. And if a demand *is* made, you'll be like Inspector Wood and say that Gary Findler's so rich he's hardly likely to be going around kidnapping people to get more money!'

'Well, yes, that *is* what I think.'

'So there you are! There's been no ransom demand – so there must be some *other* reason! Personally, I intend to start acting on the information we've got now – this evening!'

Julian asked her to explain what she meant. He was rather worried. His cousin George's adventurous ideas usually needed a bit of toning down!

'It's simple,' she explained. 'I suspect Gary Findler is behind the kidnappings, so I'm going back to my original idea of searching his yacht. As soon as it gets dark, I'll go for a stroll down in the harbour, near the *Lucy Mae's* moorings. I'll slip aboard her without being seen, and carry out a thorough search.'

'You're mad!' said Julian, alarmed. 'There are sure to be men on watch aboard the yacht – especially if your suspicions are right.'

But George was not going to be dissuaded. She stuck to her guns.

'I don't mind,' she replied. 'I'm not afraid of taking a few risks – and anyway I promise you I'll be very careful!'

'If Uncle Quentin knew –'

'Oh, leave my father out of this!' snapped George. 'This is *our* inquiry, and I'm not going to drop it now!'

But when he wanted, Julian could be just as stubborn as his cousin. He threatened to tell Uncle Quentin if she stuck to her plan. It was just too dangerous. In the end, George was forced to give in – or to *seem* to give in. She was absolutely determined to search the *Lucy Mae,* and she wasn't going to let the others stop her now that she was really on the trail. They'd soon see. And anyway, her mother and father had gone up to London for a few days.

George was a very honest person by nature, and hated doing anything on the sly. But this time, she told herself, she was driven to it by the circumstances! She waited until Anne was asleep and then slipped out of the hotel and hurried down to the harbour, followed by Timmy. Her one fear was that Gary Findler's yacht might have left.

But no – the *Lucy Mae* was still there. Not at the quayside, however, but anchored some way out into the harbour, at a distance from the other pleasure boats.

George could see the yacht distinctly in the moonlight. She was glad she was wearing nothing but shorts and a T-shirt over her bathing suit. She found a dark corner of the quay, quickly took off her shorts and T-shirt and gave them to Timmy to look after for her. Then she slipped into the dark water in her bathing suit.

George could see the yacht distinctly in the moonlight.

In her hiding place, George held her breath.

Chapter Ten

ON BOARD THE YACHT AGAIN

The sea was calm, and George had no difficulty in swimming out to the *Lucy Mae*. All she had to do now was hoist herself on board – but for a moment that looked difficult, if not impossible. She had hoped to find a rope hanging down the side of the ship, but there wasn't one. She swam all round the yacht in silence – and at last saw a place near the stern where she could climb up. It wasn't an easy climb, but George was agile as a cat, and she found just enough footholds and handholds to help her reach the deck of the *Lucy Mae*, rather breathless from the effort!

She stood perfectly still, listening. Everyone on board seemed to be asleep, so she began to move forward stealthily. The deck was deserted. There wasn't any sign of a sailor on watch – or was there? Yes – a dark shadow moving towards the bows of the boat! George thought quickly and then disappeared down a ladder leading to the interior of the yacht. Quiet as a mouse, she began exploring the passages, listening at every door and trying to find out – well, she wasn't sure just what she *was* trying to find out, but she trusted to luck to lead her to something useful.

She told herself it was a good thing she knew her way about the yacht already. 'If I'd never been on board the *Lucy Mae* before, I'd never dare to march straight into enemy territory like this!' she thought.

She reached the cabin which Gary Findler used as a study. If she searched it, she might find some sort of clue! George boldly pushed open the door and slipped into the cabin. But she had no time to begin investigating it. She heard the sound of voices out in the passage. Yes – there were two people coming this way!

George felt her heart beat faster. She looked round for a hiding place and saw a big sofa. She crawled behind it, lying flat on her front.

The voices were coming closer. The cabin door opened and then closed again. From her hiding place on the floor, George could see two pairs of feet – those of a man and a woman. They sat down on the sofa. What luck! The man's voice was that of Gary Findler and then – and George could hardly believe her ears – she recognised the voice she had first heard on the phone pretending to be Suzy. It was Isabel! Now, surely, she would find out the reason for all the kidnappings – if Gary Findler had anything to do with them.

Gary Findler was apparently filling two glassses with something. 'Well, honey, I guess we can relax a little now,' he said. 'What d'you think of my latest exploit?'

'I think you were amazingly lucky, Gary!'

'Yeah – I certainly was in luck this time!' the American agreed, chuckling. 'I knew Mark's wife was here in Southbourne – I'd seen her from a distance, and I was just wondering how I could get to be alone with her when the chance fell into my lap! Looking at the shore through my field glasses, I saw her splashing about in the water with those darn kids.'

In her hiding place, George held her breath. Luck was on *her* side just at the minute. She'd already learnt more than she could have hoped for! And she was to learn even more, because Gary Findler went on, 'Naturally I was quick to seize the opportunity. Paul was able to take the dinghy and land a little farther on, behind some rocks, and he was lucky enough to surprise Alice when she'd left the kids for a moment. It was easy to grab her and gag her without being seen – almost *too* easy!'

So George's theories had been right! Gary Findler wasn't the friendly, honest person he seemed to be at all! Feeling very excited, she went on listening.

'Kidnapping Alice was mighty near as easy as kidnapping Steve – I had *him* disappear in the middle of that party, and no one suspected a thing!' said the American.

'But Suzy Marshall gave you more trouble, Gary,' Isabel reminded him.

'Suzy walked straight into the trap herself, fortunately,' said Gary Findler, 'coming to see me like that! It was easy to keep her on board, and you phoning that Kirrin kid made everyone think Suzy had been kidnapped after leaving the yacht. I'm grateful that you were able to help with that too.'

'I'm sure you'll make it worth my while,' Isabel said.

Her voice might be low and calm, but there was a ruthlessness in it which sent shivers running down George's spine. 'There's nothing between you and the inheritance now!'

George felt her heart thumping so violently that she was afraid she might be heard!

'So I *wasn't* wrong,' she thought. 'Gary Findler *did* kidnap Steve, Suzy, Mark and now Alice. It looks as if all four of them were standing in the way of his inheriting some money from someone. I wonder who?'

During the next ten minutes, George was to find out! Because as they talked, with no idea that there was anyone who could overhear them, Gary Findler and Isabel revealed the whole story behind the kidnappings.

It was all so simple really! Over fifty years earlier, a great-uncle of Steve and Mark called Victor Harding had emigrated to America.

'Yeah, old Victor was real pioneer stock,' Gary Findler said. 'He could get what he wanted in the States, and that was the chance to make his fortune! Not that his family back in England sympathised with that kind of thing – they did all they could to stop him emigrating, forever telling him he'd be cutting himself off from them.'

'Well, I guess they forgot him pretty soon,' said Isabel.

'They sure did! But that's not so surprising, since he never sent them any news of himself. However, deep down underneath he had a lot of family feeling, and he never lost sight of them altogether. With no kids of his own, he was pleased to learn he had two great-nephews.'

'And you're sure Steve and Mark don't know what became of their great-uncle Victor?'

'Don't you fret, honey, I'm one hundred per cent sure! Otherwise I'd never have started out on these kidnappings – too risky!'

'So while Victor knows he has two great-nephews, they hardly knew he existed?'

'I have every reason to believe the family thought he'd died long ago.'

'But if they knew he's alive – and that he adopted you . . .'

Lying flat under the divan, George didn't miss a word of this fascinating conversation!

Gary Findler heaved a deep sigh.

'Yeah,' he muttered. 'When Victor Harding adopted me – why, that was about the biggest chance I ever had in my life! I was an orphan, only twelve, when he noticed me working in one of his plastics factories. He took an interest in me, maybe because my family had been English too. I owe him everything – my education, my business training –'

'And your post as manager of all his factories!'

'Yeah – everyone thinks I own them,' Gary

finished. 'The old man has a real horror of publicity – he gave me all the legal authority I needed to represent the business on my own. But in fact he's the real possessor of the vast fortune everyone believes is mine!'

'But you'll inherit it on his death,' said Isabel.

'I *would* have inherited it – all of it,' Gary corrected her, 'if my adoptive father hadn't decided to leave a share to his great-nephews back in England, dividing it equally between the three of us!'

'I can only say, Gary, I'm glad you decided not to let something so unjust happen! Why, Steve and Mark will never miss their legacies, since they don't know about them. While you – you've worked all your life to help old Victor amass more property! His fortune is all yours by rights – not just one-third of it!'

'Sure, honey, and now the old fellow's seriously ill and won't live much longer, I'm making certain!'

'But you must act fast, Gary! Don't forget, Victor's getting worse every day. When he dies, *you* must be the only one to come forward as his heir! And then you'll be really rich, and we can get married.'

Now George saw it all! Gary Findler hadn't hesitated to dispose of his rivals, so as to be the sole heir to his adoptive father's fabulous fortune. He had kidnapped Steve and Mark, who were in his way, along with Suzy, who was asking too many questions, and Alice – as Mark's wife, she might have a claim to some of the inheritance as well. And, of course, Isabel's part in the plot was now clear. Gary Findler had evidently promised to marry her.

"Gosh!' thought George, huddled in her hiding place. 'But what's happened to Suzy and the others? Can Gary Findler have murdered them? Oh no – surely not!'

What the American and Isabel said next reassured her.

'I just hope the police don't get on the track of – well, let's call them our guests!' said Isabel. She sounded worried.

'I'll be mighty surprised if they do,' replied Gary Findler confidently. 'In any event, now I've finished the business which was my official reason for visiting England, I'll be putting out to sea again pretty soon. Once back in the States, I'll tell old Victor his great-nephews are missing, presumed dead, and I'll have the documents to back me up. The old man's so weak I won't have much trouble getting him to sign a new will leaving me his whole fortune. Then, once he's dead, I'll quietly set my guests free.'

'What bothers me, Gary, is the legal action they may bring against you once they *are* free again!'

'Don't you fret, honey. Steve and the rest don't know *I'm* their kidnapper. I made sure they never saw me in person! And even if they did know, they couldn't prove anything. I could always shut their mouths, anyway.' And as Isabel seemed doubtful, he added, 'If necessary, I'd pay them such handsome compensation they'd be only too glad to be free and several thousand dollars in pocket! Don't you worry, honey, it'll be all right. We'll be married soon.'

George was stunned. It wasn't so much the plot itself, as the casual way Gary Findler was disposing of his victims in advance! He didn't seem to know much about them – George herself was sure that Steve and the others weren't the kind of people to let themselves be moved about like pawns on a chessboard. Once they were free, and they had the information she had just learnt, they wouldn't rest until Gary Findler was brought to justice. But it was a lucky thing the American was so sure of himself! If he'd been more afraid of what his victims might do, he might have thought of silencing them for good! And as for Isabel's part in the plot, George was horrified. Fancy being prepared to help a man like Gary Findler to do this and then to marry him.

George wondered where Paul fitted in, but there were more important matters, to worry about now. Her brain was hard at work.

'Just for a moment, Steve, Suzy, and Alice aren't in any danger,' she told herself. 'But I'm worried about Mark. He's injured, and being kept prisoner may make his condition worse.'

Meanwhile, Gary Findler and Isabel had come to the end of their conversation. Putting down their empty glasses, the couple rose from the sofa and left the cabin.

Before they left, however, George learned one

more detail which backed up all her theories. The hand which pushed the heavy wooden 'rock' to fall on poor Mark Turner really had been Isabel's!

What luck George had had! Now, she felt sure, she could unmask Gary Findler and his gang!

Chapter Eleven

MAKING PLANS

As soon as Gary Findler and Isabel had left the cabin, George scrambled out of her hiding place. She slipped along the corridor and made her way back to the stern of the boat, quiet as a shadow and being very cautious. Quickly, she swam ashore without being seen, retrieved her clothes and put them on over her wet bathing suit. Timmy was delighted to see her again, and they returned to the Rose Hotel together.

George changed into dry clothes, and then, after waking the surprised Anne, went to knock at the boys' door.

'Get up, you two! I'm calling a special emergency meeting of the Five.'

Timmy sat there as if he were chairman of the meeting, while George told the others about her expedition. They all exclaimed in surprise.

'I *told* you not to go!' cried Julian.

'You might have taken me with you!' Dick complained.

'To think I never heard you leave!' Anne marvelled.

'Woof!' remarked Timmy, who didn't like other people interrupting his young mistress.

Called to order by the 'chairman' like this, Julian, Dick and Anne shut up! George went on with a detailed account of her risky adventure. Julian thought her escapade had been dreadfully unwise, but he had to admit that it had certainly produced results.

'Well, thanks to you, George, we're a lot farther on now,' he said. 'We know what's behind the kidnappings at last!'

'Gary Findler must be brought to justice!' cried Dick indignantly.

'Don't you think,' suggested Anne in her soft voice, 'that the very first thing to do is to help our friends? You should tell Uncle Quentin and Aunt Fanny all about it, George!'

'But I can't, Anne – don't you remember? My mother and father left this evening to spend a few days in London with their friend Professor Hill!' George reminded her cousin. 'And as the police won't listen to us, we'll just have to deal with that gang of crooks ourselves!'

'Let's tell Ralph Morris,' Anne said. '*He'll* believe you, George. And if he talks to Inspector Wood himself, the Inspector will just have to listen and take us seriously at last!'

'Anne's right,' Julian decided. 'Let's talk to Ralph.'

It did seem to be the best solution. Since they had to wait until next morning before they could do anything, the children went back to bed, feeling really hopeful at last – but it took them ages to drop off to sleep. Morning seemed very far away!

* * *

The children had learnt to be cautious by now, so they were careful not to talk to Ralph in front of the actors, camera crew and technicians. They took the director aside and told him what they had discovered. Ralph listened with an expression of amazement on his face. He could hardly believe his ears!

'My word – I'd never have believed it!' he kept saying, looking absolutely stunned. 'Gary Findler! Who'd have thought it of him? We certainly can't have this kind of thing going on. You did quite right to take me into your confidence, children. And since your parents are away just now, George, I'll go and see Inspector Wood myself!'

Ralph immediately interrupted the shooting of the film, and left South-East Television Studios along with the Five. A few minutes later his powerful car drew up outside the police station. He and the Five attracted a lot of attention as they marched in.

But unfortunately, they were in for yet another disappointment.

Inspector Wood was away from work with a very bad cold, and the Inspector who was deputising for him was very overworked, and didn't feel at all like interfering in the delicate business of the kidnapping cases.

'I can't act on the word of a pack of kids!' he snapped.

George felt very hurt. Ralph was annoyed, too, and began telling the Inspector about the Five's adventures and all the mysteries they had solved. But it was no good, though Ralph assured the Inspector he could believe George implicitly! The Inspector had quite made up his mind not to go bothering an influential celebrity like Gary Findler – he obviously thought the multi-millionaire was above suspicion.

'Now do be reasonable, Mr Morris!' he said to Ralph. 'Put yourself in my place! I'm filling in for Inspector Wood, just for a few days, and I can't risk making mistakes. Least of all when a mistake might turn into a diplomatic incident – you never know, and don't forget, Gary Findler is an Amerian citizen!'

At this Dick exploded. He was furious with the Inspector for refusing to believe his cousin!

'We don't – and we don't forget Gary Findler is a liar and a crook too!' he cried, his voice quivering with indignation. 'He's kidnapped those three actors, and Alice Turner. They're perfectly innocent, but you won't do anything to set them free!'

'Now, now, don't get so worked up, young man! There's no call for you to try teaching me my own business!' said the Inspector, annoyed.

Realising that it was no use discussing the case with him any longer, Ralph and the children left the police station. Timmy seemed to be just as disappointed as the children. At any other time, the children would have laughed at the way his tail and ears drooped. As soon as they were outside, the children broke into an indignant chorus.

'It's a shame!' cried George. 'They won't take us seriously – just because we're not grown up!'

'Yes, I call it disgusting!' Julian agreed.

'If only Inspector Wood had been there!' said Dick. 'I'm sure things would have been different then.'

'Oh *dear*!' sighed Anne. She was terribly upset. 'And all this time Steve, Suzy, Mark and Alice are still in the power of that horrible Mr Findler!'

'Woof! Woof!' barked Timmy, sensing that the atmosphere was stormy!

'Now listen, children,' said Ralph, kindly. 'Inspector Wood's deputy isn't entirely wrong. You must realise there isn't much we can do without actual proof. So let's wait until our friend Inspector Wood is back. I'm sure *he'll* listen to me and believe what George says.'

However, the children didn't feel a bit like waiting patiently. They talked it over, and they all backed George when she suggested trying to rescue their friends without waiting for help from anyone else. They organised an expedition straight away to find out the lie of the land – or rather the lie of the *Lucy Mae*!

When the day's filming was over, the children went down to the harbour and hired a little rowing boat. Then they waited for the evening to come.

'We won't make our first move till just before midnight,' George decided. 'It wouldn't be safe to start any earlier.'

So just before midnight the Five set off in the boat. Julian and Dick took the oars, while George held the rudder and told her cousins what to do. It was a dark night, but they could just make out the shape of the *Lucy Mae* anchored a little way out in the harbour.

The rowing boat approached the dark shape of the yacht in silence. Dick found a place at her stern where they could tie up.

'Now, Anne,' George whispered, 'you stay here in the boat with Timmy, and keep watch. And be ready to cast off the painter at a moment's notice, just in case we have to beat a hasty retreat.'

Anne nodded to show that she understood. George turned to the boys.

'Julian, Dick – you come with me. I'll show you the way to climb aboard.'

The three cousins nimbly clambered up on deck, with George, who had done the climb once before, directing operations. Julian didn't mind her taking the lead, even though he was a year older – he admired her initiative! As for Dick, like his tomboy cousin, he loved a daredevil escapade.

The three children scrambled up the side of the yacht barefoot, using the hand and footholds George had found on her previous visit to the *Lucy Mae*. Coming up behind her, Julian and Dick imitated every move she made.

The three children scrambled up the side of the yacht.

Down in the rowing boat, Anne watched the other three climbing rather anxiously. All the time, she was afraid they might make some noise which would alarm Gary Findler or the members of his crew. Or one of them might slip and fall into the water with a loud splash which would give them all away!

Luckily her fears were groundless. She saw her brothers and her cousin climb safely over the rail and disappear from sight. Anne drew closer to Timmy for company, putting an arm round his neck.

'They're beginning the most dangerous part of the expedition now,' she whispered into his hairy ear. 'Timmy dear, whatever you do, don't bark! But keep your eyes open, and don't let anyone take us by surprise.'

She had only just finished talking to him when a strange noise made her catch her breath! Timmy stiffened too. It was a funny kind of scratching sound. Anne closed her eyes for a moment, and then opened them again at once – after all, George had given her a job to do, and she had to show she could do it! She must stay alert and on her guard, she thought, looking at the dark sea all round her. Then she heard the noise again, more clearly this time. Anne looked up. There was a small, white shape moving in the dark – it was only a seagull perched on the rim of a porthole, and just waking up! Its beady black eyes stared at Anne.

'Ssh, Timmy!' the little girl whispered. 'Keep quiet! We'll go chasing seagulls on the front tomorrow, but you can't chase this one now!'

Timmy buried his nose in Anne's neck, snuffling softly. It was his way of saying that he understood.

And meanwhile, up on deck, George and her cousins were getting their breath back, looking round them, and preparing for the most important part of the expedition.

Chapter Twelve

DICK GETS INTO TROUBLE

There was nothing stirring on board the yacht, but George knew there would be a sailor on watch up in the bows. She had warned Julian and Dick, and so they were all on the alert. Suddenly, Dick felt a tickle in his nose. He was panic-stricken. If he couldn't stop himself sneezing they'd be done for! The sound of one of Dick's sneezes was rather like the trumpeting of a young elephant with its tail caught between two tree trunks!

He tried to stop sneezing by pinching his nose hard. But it was no good! '*A-tishoo*!' he went.

It was a tremendous noise! But luck was on the children's side. Just at the moment when Dick sneezed, a door slammed hard quite close to them, and that covered up the sound.

A man came out on the deck. George, Julian and Dick quickly dived for shelter behind a big bundle of tarpaulin. Their eyes were used to the dark by now, so they could see that it was Gary Findler himself. He went to lean over the rail, and seemed to be absorbed in looking out to sea.

Thankfully Anne and Timmy were well out of view, in the dark shadows at the stern of the ship.

The American stayed leaning over the rail while he smoked a cigarette. Then he threw the glowing stub into the water and went back inside. George didn't hesitate for a moment.

'I'll follow him,' she whispered to her cousins. 'You search as much of the yacht as you can! We must find out if our friends are on board or not.'

And in a moment she had disappeared down the ladder and along a corridor after the figure of Gary Findler.

The light down inside the yacht was very faint. 'I expect they dim the lights at night,' George thought. 'That's a bit of luck! It will make it easier for me to follow him.'

At this late hour, she thought, the crew must all be asleep except for the sailor on watch. Perhaps Gary Findler was going round the yacht to make sure all was well on board – or perhaps he suffered from insomnia and couldn't sleep!

'If only he'd lead me to his prisoners!' George thought. 'But I'm afraid that's too much to hope for!'

Sure enough, she was just in time to see Gary Findler go into his own cabin and shut the door after him – for the night, no doubt. Too bad! George set off along another passage.

Up on deck, Julian and Dick felt rather alarmed when they saw their cousin disappear. They knew how dangerous this adventure was! However, they couldn't turn back now.

'I'm going to explore the whole deck,' Julian

101

whispered to his brother. 'That could be useful later on. You try to follow George at a distance, and be ready to step in if she gets into any trouble. But don't join her – it's better if we don't stick together.'

Dick nodded silently and set off after his cousin. Left alone, Julian decided on his own plan of action. He would go all round the deck, though avoiding the bows of the yacht because there would be a man on watch there.

So Julian stealthily explored the deck. He didn't discover very much, though he noted just where all the lifeboats and the hatchways were. He managed to avoid being seen or heard by the sailor on watch.

Coming back full circle to the point from which he had started, Julian told himself that, as Dick and George were exploring the stern of the yacht below deck, *he* ought to go below too and explore the bows. But to do that, he had to come quite close to the man on watch again. However, he set off, taking every possible precaution.

This time, unfortunately, things didn't go as well as before! Obviously the sailor wanted to stretch his legs. He suddenly turned and started walking towards Julian, just as the boy was about to dart down one of the hatches leading to the interior of the yacht. Julian was just in time to burrow hastily underneath the tarpaulin covering one of the lifeboats. The sailor stopped right beside him and lit his pipe.

While Julian, huddled up in his hiding place,

was wondering frantically how long the man was going to stay there, Dick had climbed down a ladder and found himself in a passage. But though he looked up and down it, he couldn't see George anywhere.

'Oh, blow – where *has* she gone?' he wondered.

The dim lights above him showed nothing but closed doors. There was not a sound to be heard, and Dick hardly dared to breathe. All the same, he had come on purpose to explore this yacht, so he'd better get on with it!

Cautiously, he set off.

But poor Dick didn't get far! For if the thick carpet covering the floor muffled the sound of *his* footsteps, it muffled other footsteps too.

Suddenly, just as Dick reached a point where two corridors crossed, he found himself face to face with Gary Findler!

More annoyed with himself than frightened, Dick didn't try to run away. For one thing, it was too late for that! For another, his quick brain told him it would be better to play a part which would at least gain him a little time, and might even allow George, Julian and Anne to get back to shore without giving themselves away.

So instead of appearing alarmed, Dick smiled in a rather embarrassed way. He didn't resist when Gary Findler grabbed his arm.

'What are you up to, boy? Wait a minute – I know you! Just what do you think you're doing on my yacht? Come on, out with it!'

'It's all right, sir, I can explain everything!'

Julian stealthily explored the deck.

'Just what do you think you're doing on my yacht?'

said Dick rapidly. 'I'm sorry – I *did* come aboard in secret, but I promise you I didn't mean any harm!'

'You young scoundrel,' Gary Findler gripped Dick's shoulder. Dick tried his best to stay calm. The longer he could keep Mr Findler talking, the better chance the others would have of getting away. Besides, he might learn something about where Steve and the others were hidden. He found himself being pushed into the saloon. Gary Findler sat down. Dick felt a bit like a prisoner in the dock as he stood facing the American.

'Well, young man? I'm listening!' Gary Findler said.

'I'm sure you'll understand, sir,' said Dick, looking as innocent as possible. 'You see, I had a bet with my brother and sister and my cousin – I expect you remember meeting them too.'

'A bet?' repeated the American, frowning.

'Yes, sir! I was to get on board your yacht and stay here till dawn without being found. But now I've ruined everything,' he added ruefully. 'You caught me, so I've lost my bet! That's too bad – if I'd won it, the others were going to club together and buy me a camera I've been wanting for a long time!'

While Dick was answering the enemy's questions, and trying to lull Gary Findler's suspicions, George had made a discovery which encouraged her to go on with her exploration of the *Lucy Mae*.

Quite by chance, she suddenly saw a small,

shiny object caught between the floor of the passage and the strip of carpet running down the middle of it. It was a piece of cellophane which must have escaped being picked up by the vacuum cleaner. George bent down to pick it up. Then she looked at it in surprise – the piece of paper was the wrapper of one of those special peppermints Mark liked so much! They were the kind he always ate.

It was only a short step from finding the sweet wrapper to working out that Mark either was on board, or had been on board recently – and George was quick to put two and two together.

She went back to her search, feeling keener than ever, and sure that she was on the right track now!

From time to time, she thought she heard a suspicious noise, and looked round for an emergency hiding place. But at last her search brought her to a corridor which was even darker than the rest, and which ended in front of a closed door.

George wasn't timid about trying doors, no matter what might be inside. She turned the handle very, very carefully and gently pushed. She hoped to open the door just a crack and look in. But the door wouldn't budge. It must be locked.

She was standing there in front of the door, wondering what was on the other side of it, when she suddenly heard a faint groan, followed by the muffled sound of a man's voice. Her heart began beating faster, and she could hardly suppress a cry of delight. She knew that voice – it was Mark Turner's!

'So I was right all the time!' she thought happily. 'Mark's being kept prisoner inside this cabin.'

Then she heard another voice – a woman's voice this time, answering the first one.

'Oh, my poor dear – wait a minute, and I'll make your pillows more comfortable for you.'

George could hear the words quite distinctly. She didn't hesitate a moment longer, but began gently scratching at the door with one finger-nail. Then, putting her mouth close to the keyhole, she whispered as loud as she dared, 'Alice! Mark! Hallo – it's me, George!'

Chapter Thirteen

GEORGE HAS MORE
ADVENTURES ON BOARD

The voices stopped. There was a slight rustling the other side of the door, and then Alice replied, 'Oh, George! Thank goodness – you found out where we were! Can you get us out of here?'

'I'm afraid not,' replied George, keeping her voice low but speaking as clearly as she could, so that Alice could hear her. 'We're only reconnoitring. Do you know where you are, and that you're being kept prisoner by Gary Findler on his yacht?'

'So *he* kidnapped us! But why?'

'I'll explain it all later.'

'Yes – the main thing is to get us out of here as soon as possible. Poor Mark isn't at all well. His shoulder's giving him a lot of pain.'

George was afraid she might be found if she stayed there much longer. 'Don't lose heart, Alice!' she whispered. 'Just be patient, both of you, and we'll soon be back with the police and get you out! Are Suzy and Steve in there with you?'

'No,' Alice told her. 'We don't know where they are.'

For the moment, George thought she'd learnt enough, and with a final word of reassurance she retraced her steps. She crept along very quietly. There were still two passages she hadn't explored, quite near the spot where she was at the moment. For a minute or so she wondered whether to go on with her investigations or not.

'I *could* stop now,' she thought. 'It might be more sensible – and I'm sure that's what Julian would say! But if I do go on a bit longer I may find Suzy and Steve, just as I found Mark and Alice. They'd be so glad to think that rescue was at hand!'

So she went on exploring, trying the handles of all the doors she came to and putting her ear to the keyholes. She was taking a lot of risks – and they led nowhere, because she didn't find Steve and Suzy.

'Of course, they may be somewhere quite different,' George thought. 'Yes, now I come to think of it, they probably are! Moored here in the harbour, the yacht itself isn't a very good long-term prison for people when the police are looking for them. It's much too public. Gary Findler is probably going to move Mark and Alice somewhere else, but I expect he wanted to keep an eye on Mark at first, knowing he's injured and really needs a doctor. And he shut Alice up with her husband to provide him with a nurse – very convenient for Mr Findler!'

George went on working out this theory as she tiptoed along.

Footsteps were coming her way — heavy ones!

'It may have been impossible to move Mark since he was kidnapped – I should think Gary Findler has to wait until he's a bit better before he can move the Turners to a safer hiding place. Or then again, he may be just waiting for the police to finish searching the area for Alice before he moves her and Mark to wherever he's keeping Steve and Suzy. As for where *that* is – well, finding out will be another problem!'

Suddenly, George stopped. She had come to a kind of trap-door.

'I bet that leads down to the hold!' she thought. 'And I'm sure I ought to inspect the hold, so here goes!'

However, she found nothing down in the dusty, dimly lit hold but coils of rope, materials for the maintenance of the yacht, and stocks of food and drink – with a few cobwebs thrown in!

She was about to climb up the ladder from the hold again when a sound alerted her. Footsteps were coming her way – heavy ones!

George kept her head. She saw a big, empty cardboard carton standing upside down, and quickly scrambled underneath it to hide. Lifting one corner, she peered out. Quite close to her, the trap-door had opened and two feet in plimsolls were coming down the ladder. It was one of the sailors! He looked furtive as he prowled round the coils of rope and the crates.

'Oh, if only he'd go right to the other end of the hold!' thought George. 'Then I'd have time to scurry up that ladder and make my escape without being seen.'

But the man didn't go away. Far from it – to George's dismay, he began looking in the crates near her.

'If he looks in this one, I'll be done for!' thought George. 'What on earth is he searching for?'

She soon found out. The man had come down to the hold in secret to steal some of his employer's expensive provisions! He found a bottle of some sort, and took the top off it. Raising the neck of the bottle to his mouth, he took a big gulp.

'I just wish he'd go away and take it with him,' George thought. 'Since he seems to have found what he came for, he might as well leave now!'

But the sailor didn't seem to be in any hurry to leave. He knew only too well that if his employer met him with that bottle in his hand, he'd pay dearly for his theft! So he thought it was better to stay where he was, sitting on a pile of empty sacks and enjoying the contents of the bottle. George was seething with annoyance. And she could feel a painful cramp in the muscles of her right calf. What was more, she told herself it was a long time since she had left her cousins, and Julian and Dick must be getting impatient. As for Anne, she'd be feeling terribly worried – and what about Timmy? George only hoped he wouldn't get so tired of waiting for her that he suddenly started to bark.

'That really would put the lid on it!' thought

George, very carefully shifting her position. 'Just at the moment when we've nearly solved the mystery, too. What rotten luck it would be! I told him *not* to bark, and he's a very intelligent dog, but you can never know for certain. Oh, well, I can only wait and see!'

And George had to wait for another ten minutes or more before the sailor decided to go away again. Hearing him move, she peered out and watched him by the faint light of the small electric bulb in the hold. He was screwing the top back on the bottle, and seemed to be looking round for a convenient hiding place where he could easily find it again later.

He must have known the carton where George was hiding was empty, because he came over to it, raised one corner, and pushed the bottle inside. As he did so, he nearly knocked against George's foot. She just managed to stop herself letting out a squeal! But at last the sailor walked away and climbed the ladder again, closing the trap-door after him. George heaved a sigh of relief.

'Phew!' she whispered. 'What a lucky escape!'

She hastily came out of hiding and, in her own turn, climbed the steep little ladder. She raised the trap-door very carefully and glanced out. Nobody in sight! George clambered up out of the hold and made her way back to the deck as quickly and quietly as she could.

Like a shadow, she hurried over to the stern of the yacht and leaned over the rail.

She saw Anne, Timmy and Julian below her in

113

the rowing boat, which was still tied up to the yacht itself. Swinging herself nimbly down, she rejoined them.

'So here you are at last!' whispered Julian. 'You've been taking your time, I must say! And so had Dick. He isn't back yet.'

'Did you find anything, Ju?'

'No – I wasted a lot of precious time hiding in a lifeboat so the sailor on watch wouldn't spot me!'

'Much the same happened to me,' George told him. 'I had to hide in the hold until another sailor went off and left the coast clear. But before that, I did find something – something even better than a clue! I found Mark and Alice themselves! They're here on board. I discovered the cabin where they're being kept prisoner, and I even talked to them!'

'George, that's marvellous!' exclaimed Julian, full of admiration for his cousin.

'Oh yes, it is!' Anne agreed, beaming. 'When can we rescue them?'

'Hang on!' said her brother. 'We must wait for Dick to get back before we do anything else.'

But the three children and Timmy, who was shivering in the sea breeze, waited for quite a long time, and still nothing happened. At last they began to feel seriously worried.

'I'm afraid there's something wrong,' said Anne. 'Let's go and look for him.'

'Yes,' said Julian thoughtfully. 'He should have been back ages ago. I hope nothing awful has happened! I'm going back on deck.'

'Wait a minute!' said George suddenly. 'Look

over there! The sea's very calm, and I can see the reflection of light from a porthole in the water. There – do *you* see it?'

She slightly slackened the rope tying their rowing boat up to the yacht, and the little craft swung out from the hull of the bigger one. Now they could all see the lighted porthole.

'I think that's the main saloon,' George told the others. 'I'd love to know what's going on – perhaps Dick's in there.'

'But how can you find out?' asked Julian.

'I'll show you!'

And George climbed back on deck. She had an idea! Seizing a rope, she tied it to the rail and then, clinging on to it, slithered down the side of the ship until she was level with the lighted porthole and could look in.

Her instinct had been right! Dick *was* in the saloon – but not alone! Gary Findler was questioning him. What a fix! Would Dick be able to get himself out of it?

Chapter Fourteen

INSPECTOR WOOD TO THE RESCUE

George felt even more alarmed than when the sailor had nearly discovered her down in the hold. Dick was in the power of the American! What would become of him if Gary Findler suspected he'd been spying on the yacht?

She found a foothold where she could balance, clinging to her rope. Luckily the porthole itself was open a little way, and if she listened hard, she could hear what was being said.

'Okay,' said Gary Findler drily, 'so you insist you came on board my yacht for a bet! The only trouble is, young man, I don't believe you! It'd be just too much of a coincidence.'

'I did!' Dick insisted, but his heart sank. What was happening to the others? If they came to look for him, they might be taken prisoners too. Nobody would know where they were. He didn't know that George was listening to every word!

'I think you came to steal something,' Gary Findler said to Dick. 'I'll have to keep you on board until you tell me the truth – or perhaps I'll hand you over to the police instead – I'll have to think it over.'

George had heard enough. She hauled herself back up to the deck on her rope, and then quickly climbed down to the rowing boat again.

'Quick!' she told Julian, grasping one pair of oars. 'Let's get out of here – and don't make any noise. This is serious!'

'But what about Dick?'

'Where is he?'

'Ssh!' George told her cousins. 'I'll explain later! *Please* – do as I say!'

Reluctantly, Julian too picked up his oars, and Anne cast off. Timmy sat in the bottom of the boat as it moved gently away from the yacht.

George wouldn't say any more until they had reached shore. She knew that voices carry a long way over water – and now they had to be more careful than ever!

But as soon as the three cousins and Timmy were safely on land again, George gave Julian and Anne a rapid account of what she had seen and heard. Anne was terribly upset.

'Oh, poor Dick!' she cried. 'So Gary Findler has caught him! But why didn't we try to rescue him? We must go back at once!'

'No, it would be hopeless!' said George.

'George is right,' said Julian gloomily. 'For once you've acted sensibly, old thing! If Dick's disappeared, then we have a foolproof reason now to *make* the police step in and search the *Lucy Mae* thoroughly!'

'That's just what I thought myself,' George

agreed. 'It means we can kill three birds with one stone! We'll rescue Dick, Alice and Mark – we'll unmask Gary Findler – and he'll have to tell the police where to find Steve and Suzy too!'

Feeling hopeful again, the children hurried off to the police station.

Knowing they were in the right, Julian, Anne and George honestly expected that once the Inspector deputising for Inspector Wood had heard the full story of their adventure, he would hurry to Dick's aid straight away. But yet again they were out of luck!

For a start, of course, he wasn't at the police station at all, but at home in bed! Julian told their story to the sergeant on duty at the desk, who asked if the children were trying to pull his leg, and almost lost his temper with them. At that George turned and marched out, followed by Timmy.

She went to the nearest telephone kiosk in the street outside the police station, and leafed through the directory to find Inspector Wood's home address.

'I know he's not very well,' George told herself, 'but this really *is* an emergency, and I'm sure he'll understand!'

However, poor George had a good deal of difficulty getting Inspector Wood on the line! Mrs Wood, who answered the phone, didn't seem to feel at all like disturbing her husband. But at last George heard the Inspector's husky voice – he still had a heavy cold.

'Hallo? George Kirrin is it, eh? At *this* time of night?'

'Yes, Inspector – but of course I wouldn't dream of disturbing you if it wasn't an emergency!'

And very quickly, George gave a clear and detailed account of the whole story. Inspector Wood listened carefully, without interrupting her. Then he got her to repeat it all, and asked a few questions. At last he said, 'Right, I'll call my deputy and tell him to go to the station straight away. Yes, I'll be coming myself too. I'll see you there very soon.'

Delighted with her success, George went back to her cousins. The Five – or rather the Four, as they were for the time being! – didn't have to wait too long. A little later they saw Inspector Wood and his deputy arrive within a few seconds of each other.

Yet again, however, the children were disappointed. They imagined that a few words from their friend Inspector Wood would set a big police operation in motion. But no! First, they had to answer a great many more questions, and then sign their statements. By now the sun had risen.

'We must wait to get a search warrant,' Inspector Wood explained. 'Meanwhile, you young people can go back to the Rose Hotel. We shan't be needing you any more just now,' added his deputy. 'I should think you could do with some sleep, anyway.'

But George and her cousins insisted that they ought to be there when the yacht was searched! Inspector Wood, however, wouldn't let them go with the police.

'Still, you can wait here at the station and have a nap, if you like,' he said, relenting slightly. 'And when we do get the warrant, you can come as far as the quay with us – but no farther!'

After a brief rest, when they dropped off to sleep now and then and had strange dreams and nightmares, the children woke up feeling stiff, but very ready to follow the police down to the harbour. Kind Inspector Wood had a delicious breakfast of bacon and eggs and strong tea sent in from a nearby café for them, and then they all set off.

Before the policemen got into their boat down at the harbour, the Inspector told the children, 'Now, you wait for us here – and if young Dick and your friends are on board the yacht, you can be sure we'll bring them straight back to you!'

Watching the police launch shoot off, George couldn't help muttering, '*If* Dick's on board! That's a good one, I must say! As if we'd been making it all up! Oh, blow – I do want to be over there to see what happens! Look – the boat we hired is still tied up here. Shall we take it across?'

Julian and Anne, who were very worried about Dick, soon agreed. So the children made their way back to their little boat and, for the second time in a few hours, set off for the *Lucy Mae*.

Of course, Inspector Wood and his men got there first. This time George and her cousins didn't need to take any precautions. The policemen and the crew of the yacht were far too busy to worry about anyone else, and so the children climbed on board without being noticed. George led the way, wishing they hadn't had to leave her faithful Timmy in the boat. But at least, she thought, they were about to see Dick, Alice and Mark rescued!

Chapter Fifteen

A VANISHING TRICK!

The inside of the yacht was humming like a
beehive. The police officers, with Inspector
Wood in charge, were searching all the cabins.
Gary Findler and Isabel were in the main
saloon, their faces stony, acting as if they con-
sidered the police search an insult to them as
honest citizens.

Suddenly, Inspector Wood saw the children.
'Surely I told you to stay on land?' he exclaimed in
annoyance.

Anne burst into tears. 'We're so *terribly*
worried about Dick!' she sobbed. 'Oh, please,
Inspector, find him for us soon – please do!'

The expression on the Inspector's face softened.
'Now, now, just be patient!' he said. 'Since you've
come on board after all, you might as well stay –
but don't get in our way. If you really did see your
cousin here, young George, we'll find him for
you!'

Gary Findler heard this – and realised that
George was behind the search of his yacht! He

gave her a very black look. 'This little girl has a wild imagination!' he said out loud. 'She'll invent anything to draw attention to herself. If you want my opinion, Inspector, she tells the most shocking fibs!'

George went crimson with anger, but Inspector Wood signed to her to keep quiet, and went on with his inquiries. Unfortunately, they didn't seem to be producing any results! The police officers searched the American's yacht all over, but they found no trace of Dick, and none of Mark and Alice either. All three seemed to have disappeared again – it was another vanishing trick!

And there was worse to come – the cabin where the Turners had been kept prisoner looked as if no one had occupied it for ages.

'Are you sure it was this one?' Inspector Wood asked George, after taking her down to the end of the corridor.

'Yes, positive! I talked to Alice through the door.'

'Perhaps someone was playing a trick on you?'

'No, I'm sure they weren't! And anyway, even if I'd been wrong about Alice I couldn't have made a mistake over Dick. He'd been with us! He disappeared, and then I saw him myself through the porthole, and heard Gary Findler say he was going to keep him a prisoner on board.'

Inspector Wood was still ready to believe George, but the other policemen were giving her funny looks. Dismayed and desperate, she just didn't know what to do! She felt that she'd failed all along the line. Not only had she not managed to set her friends and her cousin free – the American was coming out of the whole affair looking innocent, while she'd set the police against the Five. It was sheer disaster!

She made one more effort to convince the police officers.

'Oh, *do* believe me!' she said. 'The Turners and Dick really *were* being kept prisoner here. If they aren't here now, that's because Gary Findler suspected something after finding my cousin on board. He must have taken the three of them off the yacht in a hurry, for safety's sake – he was afraid the *Lucy Mae* would be searched!'

However, George couldn't produce any proof of what she said, and so the policemen didn't know what to think. They were angry and disappointed. As for Gary Findler, he was triumphant! He even threatened Inspector Wood, taking a very offended tone about the police search of his yacht.

'I have a lot of influence in high places, Inspector!' he said. 'You'll be hearing more about this!'

A little later, Inspector Wood and the children were back at the police station, where George firmly repeated her accusations all over again. But the Inspector's mind was somewhere else, and by now he was not in a very good temper. He simply grunted, 'This case is as tangled as a ball of wool when the cat's been at it!'

As for the other Inspector, he thought *he* could explain Dick's disappearance! 'That lad vanished of his own accord, to get himself into the headlines and have everyone talking about him,' he said. 'It's all a publicity stunt!'

Julian, George and Anne, followed by Timmy, left the police station feeling very disheartened. Back at the Rose Hotel, they had baths, slept for a little while, and then ate a good meal. By the beginning of the afternoon they were feeling rather better – rested and ready to return to the fray!

'Because we can't just sit here twiddling our thumbs and doing nothing!' said George firmly. 'And the manageress has told me my parents telephoned this morning to say they'd be back a little sooner than expected – probably this evening, in fact. So whatever happens, we must find Dick by then. Right?'

'Right!'

'Right!'

'Woof! Woof!' Timmy wasn't going to be left out.

'Good! Then this is what I suggest –'

'Half a mo!' Julian interrupted her. 'Before we do anything at all we must take a grown-up into our confidence, and if possible ask him for help. If we need a witness to back us up this time, having a grown-up there will make the police much more likely to believe us.'

George thought quickly. Yes, there was a lot of sense in what her cousin said. If the children acted on their own, they risked ending up with another disappointment. They could do much more with a trustworthy adult to support them – then, with luck, they might go one better than the police themselves!

'All right,' she said at last. 'You've got a point there, Julian. I vote we enlist an ally!'

'Ralph!' said Anne at once. 'Let's ask Ralph to help us again!'

'Just what I was going to suggest! Ralph it is! Come on, everyone – let's talk to him now!

The children found Ralph at the flat where he lived in Southbourne. As it was Sunday, he was relaxing with the newspapers and a nice cool drink. He looked surprised to see his visitors.

'Hallo there!' he said. 'It's nice to see you, but what brings you this way? And where's Dick? I hope he's not ill.'

The children told Ralph the full story of their adventures the previous night and that morning. When they had finished, he immediately jumped up.

'I'm your man, children! Yes, I certainly *do* believe you, young George! So that rascal Gary Findler is keeping our friends prisoner, is he? And he got hold of Dick too, did he? Well, we'll pretty soon get hold of *him*!'

Ralph was so indignant that they had to calm him down! But once he *was* calm and collected again, the director had a consultation with the three children, and they decided that the best person to go looking for Dick was – Timmy, with his remarkable nose! And Ralph said he would ask the television actors and the technicians working on the film to come and help with the search too.

Ralph at once made several telephone calls to summon the reinforcements. All his friends from South-East Television said they'd be happy to help the children. John Ferris and Emlyn Jones were the first to arrive, in John's car. Soon the studio van drew up outside Ralph's flat too, with the technicians in it. George told everyone the plan she had thought up – it could be adapted to circumstances – and they all agreed that it was a good one.

'Wait a minute,' said Ralph. 'I'll put this old bike in the van. It may come in useful if we find ourselves needing to go where the van can't get through.'

George looked pleased, but didn't say anything. She was anxious to be on the trail as soon as possible. She'd teach Gary Findler to keep her cousin Dick prisoner!

Chapter Sixteen

ON THE TRAIL

To start with, they all went to the place where they thought Dick would probably have been put ashore if Gary Findler had taken him off the yacht during the night. It was the spot where the *Lucy Mae*'s little dinghy was usually tied up when the big yacht herself was anchored out in deeper water.

Once there, George got Timmy to sniff one of Dick's shirts.

'Seek, Timmy! Seek Dick! Seek!'

But the dog would only sniff at the shirt itself. Then he stayed put, ears and tail drooping, and wouldn't move.

'I suppose it was too much to hope for success straight off,' said Ralph Morris gloomily. 'We might have known the American would be too clever to bring him straight back to shore here.'

'Hm,' said George. 'I think it's because he *is* so clever that he'll be keeping his prisoners within easy reach. That would mean he can act quickly to move them again if necessary.'

'The dinghy may have come ashore some-where else,' suggested Julian. 'Somewhere less public than the harbour.'

'That's what I think too,' Emlyn Jones agreed. 'Maybe we ought to go along the coast, getting Timmy here to sniff around for Dick's trail now and then.'

George thought about this idea. 'No,' she said at last. 'That would take too much time. Let's use our brains! If Gary Findler wanted to put his prisoners ashore without being seen, all he had to do was go round that headland and come in to land on the other side. So come on – follow me!'

And George was right. Once they had gone round the headland and found a spot on the other side which must be deserted at night, Timmy reacted at last! He glued his nose to the ground, breathing in and out noisily, and then wagged his tail. His sensitive nose had picked up Dick's scent! He started trotting straight ahead, along a path leading to the road along the clifftops. Here, George stopped him, and told the others what she planned to do next.

'I'll follow Timmy on the bicycle. Mean-while, the rest of you can follow me by car, but at a distance. We don't want to be noticed.'

One of the technicians took the bike out of the studio van, which was following Ralph's big car and John's smaller one. George had made sure nothing was left to chance this time!

It was an odd procession which made its way along the narrow clifftop road just outside Southbourne. George was pedalling hard up the steep slope, holding the handlebars in one hand, while the other hand held the long lead she had fastened to Timmy's collar.

Some way behind George and her dog came the studio van and Ralph's car. John had left his car behind, and was in Ralph's along with Julian, Anne and Emlyn. They didn't want *too* long a procession of vehicles – that might attract attention!

George bicycled on, trying to look as if she were just out for a ride for fun. Suddenly, Timmy left the road and turned up a narrow path. George got off the bike. The path led into a little wood. The countryside was deserted around here.

Ralph stopped his car, and he and Julian joined George. 'The van and your car will never get along this narrow path,' she said.

'Never mind,' said Ralph. 'We'll follow you on foot.'

'Anyway, George,' Julian said, 'you can't go scouting ahead on your own like this! I'm coming with you. Ralph and the others can keep a little way behind, ready to step in if we call for help.'

'I know!' said Ralph suddenly. 'Whistles – that's what you need, to summon us if necessary! There are sure to be some in the van!'

He ran back to the studio van, which had parked beside his car, and sure enough, he was soon back with the whistles, and Anne!

'I'm coming with you!' Anne announced firmly. 'Three of us won't attract any more attention than two! Come on, then!'

George couldn't help smiling. Little Anne sometimes surprised them all!

So, taking the whistles to summon the others in case of need, the cousins set off after Timmy. Ralph and his companions felt a little uneasy as they saw the children disappear among the trees.

For a few moments the three of them walked on in silence, their eyes on Timmy. 'Are you *sure* we're going to find Dick, George?' Anne asked at last, in a very small voice.

'Of course! You can see that Timmy's on the trail!'

'Ssh!' said Julian, arm outstretched to stop his sister and his cousin. 'Look!'

George tugged at Timmy's lead, and the intelligent dog, understanding her signal, stopped at once without a sound. Anne and George saw what Julian was pointing at.

There was an old farmhouse a short distance ahead of them, half hidden by the trees. The children could see it through the leaves. It seemed to be deserted.

'Hm!' said George. 'But we'd better not assume it *is* deserted. It's just the kind of place where you could hide someone, and nobody would know. The nearest neighbours must be miles away!'

'You're right!' whispered Julian. 'This isolated house is exactly where kidnapped people could be kept captive. I should think Gary Findler may well be using it as a prison!'

'Come on!' said Anne again. She could be very brave at times, and she showed it now, when she

There was an old farmhouse a short distance ahead of them, half hidden by trees.

'Here, Timmy! Dig! Go on — good dog! We'll help you.'

thought her brother Dick was in danger!

'There's no hurry,' George assured her. 'In fact, moving too fast might spoil everything. Let's make for the side of the house, away from the windows. We must go carefully if we want to rescue Dick and the others!'

'And we're not sure they're in there yet, either,' said Julian, looking glum.

'Don't be such a wet blanket! Personally, I trust old Timmy!'

Sure enough, good old Timmy was tugging impatiently at his lead, and looking imploringly at George, as if asking her permission to carry on along the trail.

'All right, Timmy, off you go! Seek! Good dog – find Dick!'

Timmy knew he mustn't bark. He was a brave, intelligent animal, and at this crucial moment he vaguely realised he had an essential part to play. George had told him to find Dick! Well, so he would – he'd lead his beloved mistress straight to her cousin.

But after going a little way the four of them had an unpleasant surprise. There was a barbed wire fence all round the house and garden. Julian was putting out his hand to see how strong the fence was, wondering if he could pull the strands of barbed wire far enough apart to let them through, when George stopped him.

'No, don't! How do we know this fence isn't connected to an alarm system? It may even be electrified.'

'What shall we do, then?' asked Anne, in dismay.

'There's only one way to get past it – we must dig down underneath it. Luckily the soil's quite crumbly. Here, Timmy! Dig! Go on – good dog! We'll help you.'

Taking care not to touch the fence, the children dug hard. In the end, they had made a hollow in the ground deep enough for them to slip underneath the fence one by one. As for Timmy, he knew all about holes and fences, and he was the first to go under this one.

'Phew!' breathed George, once they were the other side. 'I just hope nobody saw us!'

'It's not likely, with all these trees.'

'Well, here goes!'

George had taken Timmy off his lead, so that he could move about freely. Very, very cautiously, the four of them approached the lonely house. There was nothing moving. And now Julian took charge. He told George and Anne to stay where they were while he himself quickly ran across the open space which still separated them from the house.

Holding their breath, the two girls watched to see what would happen next. Nothing! George was holding Timmy's collar, and feeling him tug at it, she let him go. The dog at once made straight for a cellar ventilator and stood there in front of it, wagging his tail. Julian joined him, looked down into the cellar. Then he turned and beckoned to his sister and cousin. Had he found Dick?

George couldn't wait to know. She ran over too, and looked through the ventilator grating in her turn. But there was nothing to be seen inside except darkness – though Timmy's tail was still wagging. What had he found?

Chapter Seventeen

RESCUE AT LAST!

'The grating over this ventilator looks rather old and rusty, Ju,' said George. 'You're pretty strong – see if you can pull it out!'

Julian took hold of the grating and tugged. It gave way! George immediately wriggled in through the opening, and landed unhurt on a heap of coal. Whining gently, Timmy followed her. Then, while she was still hesitating, he dashed forward and scratched at a door. It was closed with a padlock, which stopped George for a moment, but not for long! Seeing an iron rod on the floor beside her, she used it as a lever to break the padlock, and the door flew open!

George let out a shout of delight. There were Steve, Suzy, Mark, Alice and Dick right in front of her, lined up side by side on camp beds, and all of them gagged and bound.

By now Julian had joined his cousin. He took his scout knife out of his pocket, cut the prisoners' ropes and set them free.

'At last!' cried Dick, rubbing his chafed wrists.

'Honestly, I thought you were never coming – but I knew you would in the end!'

'Julian! George! Oh, thank you, thank you!' cried Suzy, flinging her arms around both of them.

Needless to say, Steve, Alice and Mark were delighted to see them too! Julian and George were glad to hear that Mark's shoulder was feeling better now.

'I'm furious with myself for letting them kidnap me so easily!' said Steve. 'And though Suzy was very brave, she fell for Gary Findler's tricks too.'

'Well, what about me?' sighed Alice ruefully. 'Straying away on my own so that I could be carried off so easily! But it's poor Mark who had the worst time!'

'Let's hurry up and get away from here,' the practical Julian advised them. 'Findler and his men may arrive any minute, and –'

A shrill whistle interrupted him.

'It's Anne!' cried George. 'She's in trouble!'

They all ran to the ventilator, wondering anxiously what was going on out there.

Ralph Morris was the reason why Anne had whistled! Once the three cousins had disappeared, the director had been counting the minutes. Time seemed to pass very slowly! In the end he ran out of patience.

'I'm going to find out if everything is all right,' he told the others.

'But the children said they'd whistle if they were in danger,' John Ferris reminded him.

'Never mind that – I want to be closer to whatever's happening.'

And Ralph rashly set off along the path.

When he was halfway between his car and the house, Ralph suddenly saw a movement behind a bush. Two sailors from the *Lucy Mae* leaped out and attacked him! They had been guarding the place, which belonged to Gary Findler, patrolling round and round the fence. Luckily, they hadn't noticed the children and Timmy – but Ralph's heavier footsteps attracted their attention. They were suspicious, and so, following their employer's orders, they seized him.

But Anne was still on guard outside the house. From a distance, she saw the struggle, and she didn't hesitate a moment. Putting her whistle to her lips, she blew. The shrill sound alerted her cousins – and Ralph's reinforcements, who were still waiting by the van and the car.

John and Emlyn set off at a run, with the technicians after them. In a moment, Ralph was free and the sailors had been taken prisoner. Ralph was delighted to see Steve, Suzy, Mark and Alice running towards him, and there was a touching reunion! Then they all marched back to the house, just in time to prevent Isabel, Paul, and a couple of other members of Gary Findler's gang from escaping.

Looking rather embarrassed, Alice told the others that she was afraid she'd done something silly. When she was being taken away from the cabin on the yacht, she hadn't been able to stop herself telling the men who were dragging her and Mark off that she knew who their boss was.

'Hm,' said George. 'So now Gary Findler knows he's been unmasked. That certainly made your position more dangerous – and oh dear, we *still* haven't got hold of Gary Findler himself!'

'Well, we must inform the police at once,' said Julian. 'We have all the proof they could ask for now – more than enough of it!'

One of the South-East Television technicians said he'd take Inspector Wood a message. No one could say they were bothering him for no good reason this time!

And the police acted fast. While Steve, Suzy, Alice and Mark were taken back to their hotels to rest and recover, Inspector Wood had the farmhouse occupied by his men, and then he himself questioned Isabel closely.

Miserably, the young actress explained that Gary Findler would be coming to visit the prisoners at nightfall. The Inspector decided to set a trap for them on the spot. Arresting the criminals at the scene of their crime would make it easier to prove his guilt in court.

When the police asked the Five to help, of course they were delighted! Inspector Wood's trap was cleverly planned. He got five of his men to lie down on the camp beds in the cellar instead of the former prisoners. He felt fairly sure that Gary Findler wouldn't notice the difference in the dim light, or not at first anyway, and in fact that was just what happened.

When the American arrived, several policemen and the Five were standing in the cellar, hidden behind some old barrels. They waited in silence, holding their breath.

'Well, Mark, how are you?' said Findler, coming in. 'I hope your shoulder's better now. It's your inheritance I want, that's all – I may be a thief, but I'm no murderer, and I'm worried about your injury.'

'I'm very well indeed, thank you!' replied the policeman who was pretending to be Mark, suddenly jumping to his feet.

'And you've just confessed to being a thief!' Inspector Wood told him. 'Well, you know where thieves belong – locked up in jail!'

Click! Before Gary Findler had recovered from his surprise, a pair of handcuffs was snapped round his wrists. He was powerless now.

The last few days of the holiday passed like lightning for the Five. Mark soon recovered and insisted on taking over his part again. Ralph was able to finish all the shooting of his film without any further interruptions.

Steve and Suzy decided to get married at once, because they wanted the children to be at their wedding. Now that the whole story could be told the newspapers were full of it! There was a great deal of praise for the Five, and the reporters singled out George in particular, but she didn't let it go to her head!

As for Inspector Wood, the papers praised his part in the solving of the mystery too, and he was delighted!

Uncle Quentin said they could all stay at Southbourne a little longer, for a real holiday. So everyone was happy!

Everyone, that is, but Gary Findler, and his accomplices. The children learnt that Paul had been involved because he was hoping to marry Isabel. He hadn't known that Isabel was planning to marry Gary Findler once he had got all the money from Mr Harding. However, it was going to be a long time before any of *them* got married. They would soon have to stand trial, and no doubt they would all get prison sentences!

'I wonder what old Mr Harding will think when he hears how badly his adopted son behaved?' said tender-hearted Anne. 'Poor old man – I'm afraid it will break his heart!'

But Victor Harding the multi-millionaire was to die peacefully without ever knowing it – and Steve and Mark, who inherited the whole of his fabulous fortune, were glad of that. Dear old Uncle Victor – he'd never quite forgotten his family in England!

As for them, *they* didn't forget the Five. The best reward they could think of was to suggest making another television film with them in the summer. This film would feature the children and Timmy in a new adventure, based on the one they had just had!

And when the Five were shown Ralph's first film about them at a private viewing, George had quite a lot of trouble stopping Timmy from barking. He was so thrilled to see himself on television that he just couldn't help expressing his appreciation in his very own way!

A complete list of the FAMOUS FIVE
ADVENTURES by Enid Blyton:

1   Five on a Treasure Island
2   Five Go Adventuring Again
3   Five Run Away Together
4   Five go to Smuggler's Top
5   Five Go Off in a Caravan
6   Five on Kirrin Island Again
7   Five Go Off to Camp
8   Five Get Into Trouble
9   Five Fall Into Adventure
10 Five on a Hike Together
11 Five Have a Wonderful Time
12 Five Go Down to the Sea
13 Five Go to Mystery Moor
14 Five Have Plenty of Fun
15 Five on a Secret Trail
16 Five go to Billycock Hill
17 Five Get into a Fix
18 Five on Finniston Farm
19 Five go to Demon's Rocks
20 Five Have a Mystery to Solve
21 Five Are Together Again

RONNIE AND THE HAUNTED ROLLS ROYCE

JOHN ANTROBUS

When Ronnie discovers a lost, lonely old ghost in the back of his Dad's car, he decides – with the help of his best friend Ethel – to find him a job and a home.

As the ghost is frightened, and rather lazy too, this is not as easy as they expect, but the problem is unexpectedly solved when the car breaks down outside a big old house.

Also in the same series:

HELP! I AM A PRISONER IN A TOOTHPASTE FACTORY
THE BOY WITH ILLUMINATED MEASLES
RONNIE AND THE GREAT KNITTED ROBBERY

KNIGHT BOOKS